DIVINE IN LINGERIE

Lingerie #9

PENELOPE SKY

Hartwick Publishing

Divine in Lingerie

Contents

ONE

Vanessa

―――――――――――

When the truck pulled up to the house, I looked out the window to see Bones behind the wheel. He turned off the engine but kept his gaze forward, looking across the golden fields to the small hills beyond. His expansive shoulders looked too big for the truck, and he rubbed his fingers along his bottom lip as he thought to himself.

I watched him, expecting him to express his happiness in a more overt way.

A minute passed before he finally got out of the truck and headed to the front door.

I got there first and opened the door before his hand reached the handle. I looked into his face, seeing his bright blue eyes and fair complexion. Hair sprinkled his jaw because he skipped a shave that morning. Just as he looked on the night I first met him, he seemed broken. There wasn't anger in his eyes—just defeat.

I continued to stare into his face, trying to make sense of his response. My father had finally accepted the man I loved into our family, so there was no reason to be so moody. Bones was a naturally melancholy man, but this occasion deserved a smile. "What is it?"

Without taking his eyes off me, he shut the door behind him. The door clicked into place, and then the silence of the house surrounded us everywhere. Only our breaths could be heard—along with our frantically beating hearts. Bones stared at me with the same brooding expression, like he didn't have an answer.

None of this was making sense. "What happened?"

He released a quiet sigh, his nostrils flaring in the process. He finally walked past me, making sure not to touch me as he went. He moved to the couch in the living room then lowered himself, his arms resting on his knees.

I didn't even get a kiss. "Okay, you're scaring me."

He brought his palms together and slightly rubbed them back and forth. He watched his movements, more interested in his subtle fidgeting than me.

I sat beside him, feeling his heat the second I was this close to him. "My father said he would accept you.

But it seems like you've walked in here with completely different news."

He finally spoke. "Because I have."

I was already afraid when I watched him sit in the truck for an extra minute. I was afraid when he didn't kiss me when he came home. But now I was scared for a whole new reason. "Griffin?"

He turned his face my way, his bright eyes landing on mine. "He changed his mind, baby."

My eyes widened a little farther, and my chest expanded to full capacity with the breath I took. My father and I had had a long talk before he came to his decision. I told him I loved this man so much that I wasn't going to wait for his approval anymore. The conversation went well, and my family had finally moved in a new direction. "Why? How? What did you say to him?" All he had to do was be quiet and listen to my father. What did he do to provoke my father so strongly?

"The truth." He faced forward again. "He said he would give me his approval, but I had to answer one more question…"

"And what question was that?"

He sighed like he didn't want to give an answer. "He wanted to know how we fell in love. He says you're stubborn and aggressive, and there's no way you would have agreed to date me under those conditions. So he wanted me to explain how that happened. He asked the question when he already knew the answer. But he wanted to hear me say it to make sure."

I would normally be mortified that my father knew something so personal about my romantic life, but now I was too upset about his decision to really focus on that. "And you told him…?"

He nodded. "I considered lying. But I'd only gotten this far with your father because of my honesty. My integrity is the only thing he's ever respected me for. I wasn't going to throw all that away."

My palms pressed against my face, shutting out the room and the man beside me. Just when I'd thought I was getting everything I wanted, I lost it all.

"I told him I would spare your family if you gave yourself to me."

I shut my eyes even though my face was already covered. "Jesus…"

"That set him off. He pulled a gun on me, pressed the barrel right into my skull, and told me to disappear. If he ever sees me again, he will shoot me. And I believe him. The only reason he didn't kill me in his office was because of you."

"This can't be happening." I slowly pulled my palms away from my face and looked at the living room. My heart was beating so fast, but I felt somber at the same time. I felt empty inside, like there was nothing left of me to give.

He leaned forward with his forearms on his knees, his head bowed to the floor.

I sat in silence, feeling every bone in my body break. My heart hurt in a brand-new way. It was a kind of sadness I'd never felt before. Bones had told me he loved me, and I'd sent him away. But that pain was nothing compared to what I felt now. I'd done everything to make this relationship work, had done everything to keep the man I shouldn't love. But now we'd hit a dead end.

There was no moving forward.

Bones turned his face toward me, his pragmatic eyes empty of the sadness I was feeling. His carved jawline and hard cheekbones showed a masculine man who didn't feel anything at all. Devoid of emotion, as if our lives hadn't just been ruined, he stared at me like this didn't destroy him the way it destroyed me. "I'm sorry, baby."

"You're sorry?" I whispered. I swallowed the lump in my throat, but I couldn't swallow back the tears that were about to emerge. I woke up that morning happier than I'd been in a long time. The second Bones left, I pictured the way he would come home. I pictured the way we would start our lives together, the way he would ask me to be his wife. He wouldn't get down on one knee and make a romantic gesture, but he would still sweep me off my feet.

His hand cupped my cheek, and he pressed his forehead against mine. "I did everything to keep you. I proved myself to your family. I played by their rules. I made every sacrifice they asked of me. Your father was never going to accept me. He was always looking for a reason…and now he has one."

"But he said—"

"Doesn't matter. He changed his mind."

I closed my eyes, feeling the tears break the surface. "I can't believe this."

He grabbed my hand on my thigh and squeezed it.

"I just can't…"

"I know, baby."

He'd always been right. He knew we were destined to fail. There was never any hope. My family could never look past the crimes committed by Bones's father. We would always stand on opposite sides of the battlefield. "It shouldn't matter how our relationship started. The only thing that should matter is what it is now."

"He doesn't see it that way. He never will."

"It's my life…"

He shook his head slightly. "He doesn't see it that

way either. He said you'll hate him for a while, but one day, you'll thank him for this. You'll marry a good guy who will treat you right…and you'll forget about me."

"I'll never forget you. I don't want anyone else."

He closed his eyes.

I gripped his hand tighter. I felt him slip away even though he was right beside me. I felt my heart tear irreparably. I watched my entire life change, watched myself slip away. I couldn't picture myself with another man, with anyone other than Bones. I'd already planned out the rest of our lives. My family was the most important thing in the world to me, but they shouldn't have this much power over my future. I wasn't a sixteen-year-old girl anymore. I was a grown woman who knew exactly what she wanted. "I tried doing this the right way. I tried to let my family see the man you really are. I tried to bring both of you together, to accept one another. But if they can't accept us…then I don't care."

Bones opened his eyes and pulled his face away so he could look at me better. Confusion entered his gaze, affection shortly afterward.

"You're the man I want—and that's final." If I had to split the holidays between Bones and my family, I would deal with it. If I had to watch my father stare at me with disappointment and disapproval, I would accept it. If I didn't see my family as much as I used to because they couldn't tolerate the man I loved, then that was the sacrifice I had to make.

"Baby." His fingers moved under my chin. "That means a lot to me."

"I love you…" When I blinked, more tears came. "I love you more than I'll ever love another man. I can't live without you…I don't want to. I don't want anyone else to be my husband. What we have is real, intense, beautiful. I know our relationship didn't start the right way…but I would never change that."

His fingers slid down my neck, right over my pulse, and to my shoulder. His gaze shifted away from mine, and he watched his fingers slide underneath my shirt so he could feel my beating heart. He was still for a long time, like he was counting the number of beats per minute. "You're the only woman I've ever loved. And you'll always be the only woman I will ever love. There's nothing I wouldn't do for you, no sacrifice I wouldn't make. And that's why I could never let you do this."

My eyes shifted back and forth as I looked at him. My heart flushed with another surge of pain when I listened to the defeat in his voice.

"I know that's not what you want. Maybe right now it is because you're upset and emotional, but after time has passed, you'll miss your family. You'll miss the special relationship you have with your parents and your brother. Being with me will only distance you from them. Let's not forget why we did all of this in the first place…because you need your family. I would never do that to you, never take away the people who mean the most to you." His eyes lifted to mine. "I know what it's like not having a family. It's depressing, lonely, and empty. I wish my mother were still alive. I wish I had a brother or sister. I wish I had someone…but I don't have anyone. As much as I want you, as much as I love you…" He shook his head. "I never want you to be alone…not even with me."

"They would still be my family——"

"It wouldn't be the same. You can always find another man to replace me, but you'll never replace your family."

"I don't want to replace you either…"

"Neither do I." He kept his voice steady even though I was covered in tears. "But we don't have another choice. This is how it has to be." He pulled his hand out of my shirt before he dug it into the back of my hair. He regarded me with a hard expression that was slightly tinted with sadness.

"No…"

He pressed his lips against my forehead and

brought me into his chest. His powerful arms locked around me, and he held me close, his body warm and hard. His chin rested on my forehead, and he breathed with me.

I cried into his chest, unable to stop the tears. I'd been with other men who were handsome, successful, and interesting, but not a single one compared to this man. I loved him with all my heart, loved him even when I knew I shouldn't. It was the kind of love I couldn't explain to another person. I could argue with my father forever, but he would never understand how I felt about this man. He claimed he loved my mother in a way words couldn't express, but that love wasn't different from what I had with this man. "I can't do this."

Every time he took a breath, his chest expanded against mine. I could feel the shivers that rocked his body, the hints of emotional instability. I could feel the slight tremor of his hands, feel his heart crack inside his powerful chest. He didn't say a single word, but he didn't need to. I knew he was just as broken as I was. Even more broken. "Neither can I."

I STILL HADN'T ACCEPTED the truth.

That this was over.

Bones and I didn't speak of it again. We didn't establish when he would be leaving or how we would say goodbye. Neither one of us wanted to deal with it, so we both decided to ignore it.

But we couldn't ignore it forever.

My father put a gun to his head and ordered him to disappear. But if my father showed up on my doorstep to make sure Bones left, I wouldn't open the door. It would be the first time in my life that I would tell my father off.

But I knew he wouldn't come. I knew he respected my privacy…to some degree.

We lay in bed side by side that night, my leg hooked over his waist while his face rested close to mine on the pillow. Instead of closing his eyes and drifting off to sleep, he chose to stare at me instead.

Now that my relationship with Bones had an expiration date, all I could do was cherish every single moment I had left. He would walk out that door soon, and I would never watch him walk back through it. My nights would be lonely, and all I would have to get me through the darkness were our memories.

I couldn't imagine being with anyone else. I couldn't picture myself married with a family. I couldn't picture my future when this man was all I ever wanted. Would I ever fall in love again? Was there a man out there who could compete with the man who had claimed my heart, body, and soul?

His hand slid up my back and underneath my hair. His fingers touched me lightly, his caresses gentle. His eyes never left my face, and instead of reflecting the pain that burned in his heart, his hands showed his depression. They shook a little, tiny vibrations that were almost undetectable.

My hands kept gripping him, making sure he was really there. I didn't want him to slip away, to leave me without saying goodbye. Bones was that kind of man, the kind who slipped out in the middle of the night so I wouldn't have to watch him go. That was the last thing I wanted. "Don't leave without saying goodbye." Watching him walk out of my life would be the hardest thing I'd ever had to do, but it was better than missing that moment altogether.

His eyes softened. "Alright."

We still hadn't discussed when he would be leaving. We hadn't discussed anything. Would I stay at the house when he left? Would he return to Milan or Lake Garda? If I wanted to stay in Tuscany, I would have to stay with my parents, but that was the last place I would go. I didn't hate them for the decision they made, but I certainly didn't want to look at them right now.

"I want to stay as long as I can…but I know that's not good for either of us."

The longer he stayed, the more I dreaded the moment he would leave. Anticipating that terrible moment made me hurt all over. Just thinking about it stopped me from breathing. I would watch the love of my life walk out that door, and I wouldn't stop him. I was saying goodbye to the greatest love I'd ever known.

"So, I'm going to leave tomorrow." Bones was handling this situation much better than I was. While I spent my time crying, he kept his stoic expression. He wasn't angry or sad, almost indifferent. He'd never been an emotional man, but he'd always been passionate. That intensity disappeared the moment he left my father's company. It was the first time he'd seemed so defeated.

"No." My palm went to his chest, resting right over his heart. "No, that's too soon. I'm not ready."

"You'll never be ready, baby."

"No." My voice came out firmer, sterner than I'd ever been before. My breathing was haywire, and I could barely keep myself calm. Regardless of when he left, I wouldn't be ready for it. But I certainly wasn't ready for him to leave that soon. "Just no, alright?" I pressed my face into his chest so I could find comfort in his warmth and strength. I didn't want him to look at me, to see how weak I'd become. A part of me regretted loving him in the first place. My instincts had told me it would end this way, but I'd made the mistake of falling madly in love with him anyway.

"Alright." He brushed his lips against my forehead. "Then the day after."

My eyes were closed, and I inhaled his scent. "How can you be in such a hurry to say goodbye to me?"

"That's not how it is, and you know it."

"Seems like it."

"The longer we stretch this out, the more painful it's going to be."

"Doesn't seem like you're in pain at all…" It must have been the anger over the situation talking, but now I was spitting out anything that came to mind. I was furious and frustrated that this was happening, that we'd come so far only to fail.

"You know I am."

"Then why am I the only one who's a mess?"

He ran his hand down my hair and along my spine. "Just because I'm not a mess on the outside doesn't mean I'm not a mess on the inside."

WHEN I WOKE up the next morning, he was gone.

He was nowhere in the house, and there wasn't a note.

I immediately panicked, thinking he'd left without saying goodbye even though I asked him not to.

But then I remembered he wouldn't lie to me, especially not now. I didn't have a clue where he was or why he'd slipped out so early in the morning, but in my heart, I knew he would come back.

I skipped breakfast because I wasn't hungry, and I sat at the kitchen table with a bottle of his scotch. Instead of having coffee, I decided to hit the booze. I drank from the short glass as I stared at the large bottle filled with amber liquid.

I was so heavy with sadness I didn't know how to process it. It was so painful that it didn't seem real. I couldn't believe Bones would leave tomorrow morning.

And I would have to move on.

He would go back to his lifestyle, killing for cash and screwing prostitutes. He would close up again, turning his back on the world in favor of solitude. My painting would hang in one of his rooms so he would never forget my face. The years would pass and he would slowly forget about me, but he would never forget I was the only woman he'd ever loved.

I would lick my wounds for a long time, cry over the man I couldn't have. But one day, I would stop dragging my feet on the floor and put myself out there again. Maybe I would meet a man I liked, but I didn't believe I would meet one I loved. My family would be happy about the new man in my life, but in my heart, I would always want the man I couldn't have. Despite how much I loved my father, I would always resent him for taking Bones away.

I drank the scotch and sat in the silence of the small villa. When Bones left tomorrow, I would probably stay here until I decided what to do. The only other place I could call home was my apartment in Milan. That place was heavy with memories of Bones, so I couldn't stay there. With the money I'd made from my paintings, I should be able to get a new place. But did I want to stay in Milan? My plan had been to return to Tuscany and live in Florence, but now that I was angry with my father, I wasn't sure if I wanted to be so close to them right now.

I didn't belong anywhere.

An hour later, the front door opened, and Bones's heavy footfalls sounded against the tiled floor.

I stared at the half empty bottle of scotch, my stomach warm from all the booze I'd just consumed.

Bones stopped in the kitchen, staring at me with his irritated gaze.

I didn't look at him. "Where were you?"

He held his silence, his disapproval filling the air. After pausing at the kitchen counter, he walked to the table and snatched the bottle from the surface. He examined the contents, calculating how much I'd drunk. "Don't pull this stunt, Vanessa. You're better than that."

"I'm better than that?" I asked incredulously. "I can't even remember a time when I've seen you drink water."

"Because I never have." He took the glass away from me and downed the rest of it. "I understand you're upset, but don't go down this path. You're better than this, and I expect more from you."

I gave him a glare. "Then don't expect anything from me."

"Too bad," he snapped. "I always expect the world from you." He pulled out the chair beside me and sat down, his body pivoted toward me. "I know this is shitty, baby. But you're going to move past this. One day, you're going to meet a nice guy, fall in love, and forget about me."

His words infuriated me so much that I couldn't think straight. Without thinking twice about it, I pulled my hand back and slapped him hard across the face. I hit him with enough force to turn the skin red. "Don't say that to me."

He turned with the hit, clenched his jaw, and then gave me a terrifying glare.

"I can't believe you think our love is so trivial."

"I don't. I just don't want you to lose yourself over this. Where's the strong woman I fell in love with? Where's the woman who doesn't shed a tear over a man? That's the woman you need to be right now. I don't want you to be miserable. I know it sucks right now, but there's a future for you. You're in pain now, but you won't always be. When I walk out that door, I want to know that you're going to be alright."

"Be alright?" I whispered. "How can I be alright without you?"

His eyes softened, but only for a moment. "You can do it, baby. You know you can call me if you need anything. I don't care if you have a husband or kids. I'll always be there if you need me."

"I don't want to do this…"

"I know," he said quietly. "But it's happening. I need you to keep yourself together."

"I guess I'm not as strong as you."

"No." He gripped my wrist and gave it a squeeze. "You're stronger." He brought my hand to his mouth and placed a kiss right over the veins. "I know this hurts, but I know you have the strength to pull through it. I don't want you to suffer. I want you to be happy."

"You want me to love someone else?" I asked incredulously. "To find a nice guy like my father wants?"

He stared at my hand for a long time, pondering my question. He lifted his gaze again. "I want you to be happy, baby. If I can't have you, I don't want you to be alone. I would much rather picture you with a family like you've always wanted instead of depressed and alone because we can't be together."

My eyes softened, accompanied by a hint of tears. "Where were you?"

He looked away again. "I'll tell you tomorrow."

"Why can't you tell me now?"

"Because." He turned his gaze on me, this time stern.

I didn't bother asking any more questions because I knew I wouldn't get an answer. "What do we do now?" I wanted to appreciate every moment we had left, but I was too upset to feel spontaneous or happy. Normally, we'd be making love or staring into each other's eyes. But neither one of us was in the mood for that.

He pulled back his sleeve and looked at his watch. "I have less than a day left with my woman. I know exactly what I want to do."

THE SEX WASN'T good like it usually was. Knowing every kiss and thrust were final took all the enjoyment out of it. All I could think about were the nights I would be spending alone, remembering the evenings when things were good between us. I pictured him with the women who would follow after I was gone. I imagined the men I would date then dump. My hands moved through his short hair and down his muscular back, but it wasn't the same as it used to be.

I was too heartbroken.

Bones wasn't the same either. His lovemaking was slow, full of abrupt stops, like he was being hit with the reality that this heartbreak was inevitable. He was a powerful man who could control anything, but he couldn't stop the sun from rising.

No one could.

All of our heat and passion had been stripped away, replaced by anger, fear, and sorrow. We were just ghosts of who we used to be.

We lay in bed together once the sun rose. The light slowly filled the bedroom as the world came to life once more. Tears constantly burned behind my eyes, but I never let them fall. I treasured the feeling of his hard chest underneath my hand, the way his blue eyes darkened when he stared at me. I was trying to capture everything, to keep it in my memory for years to come.

I should want to forget about him to make this all easier, but Bones was definitely a man I never wanted to forget.

He was the love of my life.

Hours passed, and he stared at me with his handsome gaze. His eyes were empty, but his jaw was tight and his muscles rigid. He'd never been the kind of man to wear his heart on his sleeve, to display his emotions like a painting. To a stranger, it would seem like he was handling this breakup well. It might even seem like he was indifferent to it altogether.

But I knew that wasn't the case.

He leaned over me and pressed a kiss to the skin over my heart. He let his lips linger, clinging to my warm skin before he pulled away. The sheets were kicked back, and he rose from the bed.

I knew what was coming.

Moving at a slow pace, he pulled on his clothes. First, it was his boxers and then his jeans. His t-shirt came next, along with his shoes.

I sat up in bed and watched him, the blankets held against my chest. It was time for me to get up and put my clothes on, but my body was too weak to move. Every breath hurt my chest, like I was breathing in poisonous gas.

Bones turned back to me, his hollow eyes full of

sympathy. He watched me for a long time, silently demanding me to rise and get dressed. He wanted me to be stronger than this, to not be a wreck once he walked out that door. Despite my pain, he expected the most out of me.

I finally got out of bed.

The moments between getting ready and moving to the front door were horrible. My heart was beating fast with adrenaline, and my hands were shaking with the same tremors that Bones had. The love of my life was about to walk out forever. I would probably never see him again, only have his memory for comfort.

He already had his bags packed. He probably did it in the middle of the night to spare me the pain of watching him gather his things. They must already be in the truck because he didn't carry them with him.

I followed him to the front door but stopped before I reached the threshold. "I can't do this…" Tears were already starting to break past the flimsy barrier I was erecting. I'd always prided myself on being stronger than the average person, but all that confidence failed me. This was the hardest thing I've ever had to do, and I didn't think I could see it through. I'd been captured by a psychopath and I'd been shot in the arm, but those experiences didn't leave me crippled the way this did.

I'd rather be shot a million times than have to say goodbye to this man.

He slowly turned around, the disappointment in his eyes. "You're stronger than this."

"No, I'm not," I whispered. "I can't turn off my heart the way you can."

His eyes narrowed, his jaw clenched a little harder.

"This is the hardest thing I've ever had to do. I can barely breathe right now…"

"But you will do it, baby. You have your whole life ahead of you."

"What kind of life will that be without you?" I snapped. "There will never be another man out there who will make me feel the way you do. Anytime I'm with someone, I'll only think of you. And even when I'm not, I'll still think of you. You aren't just some man that I'm sleeping with—"

"I know." His voice turned gentle despite the irritation in his voice. "I know how hard this is because I'm standing here with you. The idea of moving on after I've had something so great…sounds impossible. I thought my life was about to change. I thought I was going to settle down and say goodbye to the life of loneliness I used to live. But now I have to go back to it…as much as I don't want to. My life will be bleak, a series of reckless decisions without consequence. But Vanessa, you have so much more to live for. Don't go weak on me, not now and not ever. Hold your head high, be strong, and don't lose yourself. The last thing I want is for you to be miserable, to make mistakes you'll regret because of sadness. Take it slow, pick up the pieces, and then find the right man who can replace me, someone who will love you, provide for you, and protect you."

The second I blinked, two tears streamed down my cheeks. "How can you say that to me?"

His jaw clenched tighter.

"How can you tell me to be with someone else so calmly?" My voice broke.

"It's easy." With stiff shoulders, he stared at me with the same intensity as before. "If we can't be together, the next best thing is you being happy. I'm not a sadist. I don't get off on the idea of you being miserable forever. I want you to end up with a husband and kids."

I crossed my arms over my chest and felt more tears stream down my face. "I don't even want to think about that right now. I don't want to think about you with some other woman. If you think I'm going to stand here and encourage you to get married and have your own family…that's never going to happen. Maybe I'm selfish and petty, but it hurts too much to say those things. And it hurts even more to hear them."

He broke contact and dug his hand into his pocket. "When I told you I loved you, I meant it. That means I want you to be happy—even without me. When you meet someone you like, I don't want you to push him away because of my memory. Loving you means I have to do the right thing, even if my heart is telling me otherwise." He pulled a folded-up envelope from his pocket and placed it in my hand. "Open this when I leave."

I gripped it in my fingers and felt something hard inside, like a key. "What is it?"

"Just open it when I leave." He opened the front door, taking this goodbye to the next stage.

More tears fell. "I can't do this…"

"Yes, you can." He turned back to me, his expression as stoic as ever. I was fighting for sanity while he was perfectly calm. Even when a gun was pointed at his skull, he didn't flinch. He never panicked despite the severity of the situation. This moment was no different. It didn't affect him at all. "I know you can."

"This isn't as easy for me as it is for you."

"Baby." He slid his hand around my waist, and he looked down into my face. "Trust me, it's not."

I pressed my face against his chest and cried, my hands gripping his biceps as tightly as possible so he couldn't walk away.

He rested his chin on my head and stood there with me, listening to me sob and feeling me soak his t-shirt.

In that moment, I hated my father. I hated what he'd done to me. I hated myself for walking down that alley in Milan at the wrong time. My love for this man was so powerful that it cursed me in the end, and a part of me regretted it. If I'd just had a meaningless relationship with Mateo, I wouldn't be feeling this way. If I'd never loved so fiercely, I wouldn't feel this loss so fiercely.

Bones cupped my cheek and directed my gaze on him. "I love you. Always will."

I locked my arms around his neck, and I kissed him, kissed him for the last time. "I love you…" Our kiss was mixed with tears, my words lost in the sorrow. "You're the love of my life."

He kissed me a little harder, his fingers digging into my hair. Our tongues moved in sync as our lips came together and broke apart. His hand shook slightly against me, his passion and emptiness combining.

Then he abruptly pulled away. He turned around without looking at me again. He was out the front door in less than a second and then headed to his truck in the driveway. He was careful not to look at me, to see the devastated expression on my face before he left our relationship forever.

I watched his shoulders shift as he moved, watched him approach his truck and prepare to leave my life. Since the moment he'd come home from meeting my father, he'd been nothing but calm. He accepted my father's judgment without argument, and even when I wanted to be with him anyway, he rejected the idea. This separation ruined my life, but it didn't affect him in the same way. He was either incredibly strong or incredibly heartless.

He told me to marry someone else without a single hint of pain.

How could he say that to me?

He arrived at the truck and opened the door.

"Griffin." I was just in one of his t-shirts with bare feet, but that didn't stop me from crossing over the threshold and stepping onto the gravel of the driveway. The small rocks hurt my feet, but that didn't stop me.

He kept his hand on the open door but didn't turn around.

"Griffin." My feet crunched against the gravel as the early morning light stretched across the golden fields. It was still dawn, and not a single car was on the road. The birds were singing, welcoming spring. It was a beautiful day, but that beauty wasn't strong enough to diminish this painful moment. I stopped behind him, staring at his muscular back in his t-shirt.

"Don't make me look at you again."

"I just…" I didn't want to leave things this way. All I'd done was yell at him for the things he said and cry, but I'd never told him I wanted him to be happy. He could say it to me, but I couldn't say it to him. This was the last chance I would ever get. "I want you to be happy too…" That was the most I could say. That was the only blessing he would ever get from me. He could interpret it in whatever way he chose.

He took a deep breath but still didn't turn around. "Griffin…"

He finally dropped his arm from the car door and rotated, coming face-to-face with me. The strong man I saw just a moment ago had disappeared. His detached expression was gone, his indifference no longer evident. With wet eyes showing a tint of redness, he wore an expression I'd never seen before.

The look killed me, put a bullet right in my heart. His sadness destroyed me, made me feel worse than I already did. The strongest man I'd ever known had been reduced to brokenness. Tears burned in my eyes even more, and the sobs started to rack my body.

He kept control of his emotions better than I did, didn't let a single tear fall. But the buildup of moisture was there, the redness in his eyes apparent. The skin around his eyes started to become puffy. He was too proud to cry, but not strong enough to hide the evidence of his impending tears. He'd been shot dozens of times, had suffered more than any person I'd ever known, and not once did he cave to the sadness. But this moment was the one that broke him. He cupped my cheeks with both hands and pressed a kiss to my forehead. His lips lingered a long time, warm and soft. The hair from his jaw brushed against me, making me think of all the times it happened before. "Goodbye, Vanessa."

TWO

Vanessa

After Bones left, I didn't open the letter.

Watching him drive away and disappear down the road broke me in a whole new way. I immediately went to bed, lay in the sheets that I shared with him every night. The bed smelled like him, and in some ways, it felt like he was still there.

I stayed in that spot for a long time. I cried on and off. Sometimes, I fell asleep. When I woke up, I cried again. I became a woman I didn't recognize, someone so weak and pathetic. Before Bones, a man had never had such an intimate hold on me. I didn't refrain from walking away if I didn't like him. If he had the audacity to say something insulting, I didn't hesitate to insult him back. I never lost sleep over a guy, and I certainly never cried over one.

But Bones was different.

Over the span of a few days, I hardly moved. It wasn't until I got a serious migraine that I realized I hadn't eaten in several days, so I forced something down my throat. My phone never rang, but I didn't expect Bones to call me.

He never would.

We both knew that would make this so much harder.

I wondered where he was. He'd probably returned to Lake Garda, his favorite retreat in the world. The snow was long gone, but it was still his favorite hideaway. It was preferable to his apartment in Milan, which still had all of my things.

After I showered and had a small breakfast, I finally opened the letter Bones gave to me. I hoped it wasn't a heartfelt goodbye because I couldn't go through that again. Bones had never been big on words, so I doubted he had much to say.

I read through the words, but I squinted in confusion. It was just an address in Florence along with a single iron key. There was no message. He didn't even sign it. I turned it over to make sure I hadn't missed anything, but there was nothing there.

What was at this address?

I didn't have a car, so I called a cab and got a ride

into Florence. My parents had a lot of extra cars at the house, but I refused to ask them for anything. My anger and resentment would last a long time. As a Barsetti, I was stubborn and emotional. Just like my father, I had a poor temperament. If I came face-to-face with him right now, I would have nothing nice to say.

The cab pulled up to a two-story building in the center of town, and I stepped out and checked the address one more time. I was in the right place, so I looked at the large window in front of the building. It seemed to be a shop of some kind.

Why did Bones give me the key to a shop?

I walked to the front door and inserted my key, expecting it not to work. But it slid in perfectly, and after a turn, the door opened.

I stepped inside and my shoes tapped against the hardwood floor. The walls were plaster-white, and the large windows allowed natural sunlight to enter the large, open room. I took a look around and didn't see any distinguishable features that answered the question lingering in the back of my mind.

On the table was a single note, along with two sets of keys. I picked up the letter. In handwriting I'd never seen before, Bones had written his message.

I KNOW you said you wanted to do this on your own, but you know I never listen to you. I wanted to leave you with something, something that would bring you joy every single day. I hoped I would be the man to take care of you, to give you the life of luxury you deserve. So let me do this. Let me have a piece of you forever.

This is your gallery.

Upstairs is your apartment. I've left the paperwork of ownership on the coffee table. The gallery and the apartment are both yours.

And I got you a car.

Yes, I know you're pissed. But you look cute when you're pissed, so that's fine with me.

Take it all, baby. And be happy.

-GRIFFIN-

HE DIDN'T SAY he loved me, but I knew that would be too hard for him. I wasn't sure when he'd written this letter. Maybe he stopped by here after he left the house. I wiped away the tear that had dripped down my cheek and carefully folded the letter before I placed it in my purse. On the table were two keys. One was for the apartment upstairs, and the other was for the car. I hit the black button and heard the car outside release two quick honks.

I looked out the window and saw the white SUV at the curb.

Of course, he got me an enormous car I didn't need.

I wasn't angry about any of it. In actuality, I was touched by the gesture. I'd never needed his money, but I was more than happy to receive such a meaningful gift. Time would pass and our lives would change, but I would never forget how I opened this gallery and who was responsible for making it possible.

Now it would seem like he was always with me.

I left the gallery and ventured upstairs to the apartment. It was a two-bedroom place with a nice living room, full kitchen, and two bathrooms. The living room had a large window that looked across the city, and sitting there were an easel and a stool. A stack of blank canvases leaned against the wall, and all my art supplies were waiting for me.

He must have moved everything here.

I examined the plush couches and the coffee table then noticed the large painting on the wall.

It was the painting I'd made of him. He was standing beside the water in Lake Garda, only his backside visible. He looked across the water, his powerful shoulders wide and intimidating. It was quiet, cold, and beautiful. It was a snapshot of the night we met, the night that changed my life forever.

He got it for me. He knew I would want to look at that painting every single day.

To remember the man I fell so madly in love with.

THE BEST WAY TO combat the pain was to keep busy. So I worked in the gallery downstairs, added a new coat of paint to the walls and set up the floorplan to display my paintings. I wanted my work to have an elegant atmosphere since my paintings were rich with emotion. I wanted people to connect with my artwork, so they needed to connect with the gallery just as much. Instead of making it dark and moody, I brightened it up, hung two chandeliers in the center of the ceiling, and added a few art lights. I didn't know anything about wiring through the roof, but I didn't let that stop me. I had the money to hire a professional, but I needed something to do. The longer it took, the better.

I'd just unrolled a new rug to go in the center of the room when my phone started to ring.

My heart always hoped it would be Bones, but I had to remind myself it never would be.

I would never talk to him again.

I pulled out my phone and saw my father's name on the screen.

Anger, ferocity, and disappointment flashed through me in a split second. The logical part of me knew my father was just trying to protect me, but I wasn't logical at the moment. I was an emotional wreck, devastated that I'd lost the love of my life. My father was the only man to blame for this heartbreak. I considered not answering, but I knew there was never a time in my life when my father didn't take my calls.

So I answered. My silence was my only greeting.

My father was quiet too, sitting on the line. He must be able to detect my anger through the hush because he didn't start speaking right away. "*Tesoro*—"

The second I heard his masculine voice, the rage exploded inside my chest. It was the only time in my life when I thought I hated my father. I despised him for causing this pain. I despised him for taking away the love of my life. I despised him for being so hypocritical. "I'm not ready to talk to you." For the first time in my life, I hung up.

I hung up on my father.

I shoved the phone into my back pocket and got back to work, forgetting the phone call happened in the first place. In my heart, I knew I didn't really hate my father. The rational woman inside me knew he was putting my best interests first. But right now, I didn't care about that. I saw him as the enemy.

I got back to work.

TWO WEEKS PASSED, and I spent that time perfecting my gallery and my apartment. Once the gallery was ready for business, I realized I didn't have any artwork to display. I'd given my pieces to my parents to put up at the winery.

So now I had to get back to work.

It was hard to get back into painting because I'd been too depressed to feel creative. It showed in my work. My pictures were moodier, with darker colors and sensations of isolation and loneliness. I tried to force myself to make paintings that were popular with my customers, but I couldn't bring myself to do it.

Instead, I painted images that meant something to me.

I painted Bones.

He was everywhere in my paintings, his face never visible. I painted him lying in my bed, standing underneath the stars on a dark night, and working at the winery. I painted the places we'd been together, from Lake Garda to Milan.

Over the course of a few days, I made five different pieces.

I wasn't sure if anyone would buy them. Most subjects in paintings were beautiful women, whether they were naked or dancing. It was rare to see a beautiful man as the focal point in an image.

But that didn't stop me from trying.

I displayed them in my gallery, the first artwork that would be available for sale. I wrote down the prices I thought they were worth, making them expensive on purpose so no one would buy them. It was hard to imagine someone taking these artworks, the pictures of my memories, and putting them in their home. A part of me didn't want to let them go.

I never wanted to let them go.

The front door opened, and my first customer walked inside. It was the first day that I'd been officially open for business, but I didn't expect anyone to stop by. I didn't market my gallery or tell a single person that I was open. My family didn't know about any of it.

I was basically on a different planet.

I heard heavy footfalls against the hardwood floor, so I knew it was a man who'd walked inside. I was adjusting one of my paintings in the corner, so I didn't see him right away. Once the image was straight, I turned around to see my first potential customer.

But I came face-to-face with my father instead.

He was dressed in dark jeans and a black t-shirt, his tanned skin complemented the dark colors he wore. With jet-black hair and green eyes, he possessed the masculine version of some of my features. His eyes settled on me, and instead of being angry that I'd hung up on him, he looked like the one who'd just had his heart broken.

The anger I felt for him diminished when I saw his expression, when I remembered how much he loved me. He knew I hated him in that moment, but that didn't stop him from pitying me, from feeling the same heartbreak I did.

I crossed my arms over my torso, my heart racing in my chest. I had no idea how he'd figured out where I was, how he knew about this gallery. I wondered if he and Bones had had a conversation, but after my father pulled a gun on him, that didn't seem likely.

He stared at me with his hands in his pockets, his eyes hesitant because he didn't know what my reaction would be.

I wasn't sure what my reaction would be either.

He stayed quiet for a long time, giving me the chance to speak first if I wanted to.

But I didn't have anything to say. Right now, I didn't care about anything. All I cared about was the insufferable depression that had sunk in all the way to my bones. I didn't want anyone's company. All I wanted was to be alone.

My father turned to one of the paintings, the one of Bones working at the winery. With the backdrop of the endless vineyards and the cobblestone pathways between the buildings, it seemed like a beautiful day in Tuscany. Bones was passing between the buildings, carrying a barrel of wine to the storage room. My father stared at it for a moment before he turned back to me. "Beautiful gallery."

My arms tightened over my chest, and hearing him speak made me realize how upset I still was. I didn't want to make small talk and pretend nothing happened. But I didn't want to have an honest conversation about what really happened either. "I'm still not ready." I lowered my gaze, unable to look my father in the eye. I didn't want to see his sadness. Despite how much he'd hurt me, I didn't want to hurt him.

My father stayed still, his hands in his pockets.

When my bravery returned, I looked at him again.

His expression hadn't changed, but his eyes hinted at his sadness. He breathed a deep sigh, his frustration and heartbreak evident. "*Tesoro*, please don't hate me."

"I don't hate you," I blurted. "But that doesn't mean I want to talk to you."

His eyes flinched, like my words packed punches. "Your mother and I are worried."

"I just lost the love of my life. Don't expect me to feel better in a few days."

"Vanessa, it's been three weeks…"

I had no grasp of time. Sometimes I slept all day, and sometimes I didn't sleep all night. I didn't eat at regular times, and I didn't even know what day of the week it was. The last three weeks felt like a painful blur. I wasn't sure how I'd lived that long without speaking to Bones, without looking at his pretty blue eyes. How much longer would I feel this way? Would a pain this intense ever end? "I guess I lost track of time…" I rubbed my upper arms with my palms, fighting a chill that hadn't descended. "How did you find me?"

"I never lost you."

He'd probably been watching the house since he ordered Bones to leave. He'd followed me all the way here and kept an eye on me from a distance. This whole time I thought I'd been alone, but I'd never really been on my own. "He bought me this gallery… gave me an apartment and a car. I never asked him for those things. I've never wanted his money. But he wanted to give me something before he disappeared."

My father held his indifferent expression, Bones's gifts meaningless to him.

"You never really gave him a chance, did you?" My anger started to rise again, my bitterness burning in my blood.

"You know I did."

I shook my head, unsure if I could believe him.

"I know you're upset right now. I know you're hurting, and that hurts me. But one day, you'll realize this is the best thing that ever happened to you. You deserve a lot more than that man, and I'm not going to let you settle for anything less than someone who's perfect."

"There's no such thing as the perfect man. Even if there were, that's not what I want. I love him for who he is, all of his strengths and flaws. And he loves me despite all the baggage that comes along with me. Why would I want a perfect man when I have the perfect love?"

Speechless, he just stared at me.

"You made the wrong decision."

He shook his head slightly. "No, I didn't. And I won't change my mind. You're lucky I didn't kill him. The only reason I didn't was out of respect for you. But if I cross his path again, I won't hesitate."

"You've got him all wrong…"

"A man who forces a woman to sleep with him is

fucking trash." His jaw clenched, and his eyes darkened with threat. My father and I never talked about this stuff, but that discreetness was long gone.

"He didn't force me—"

"He didn't give you a choice. You either had to comply, or he executed your whole family. What other option did you have? You think I would ever walk you down the aisle and give you away? To him? Over my dead body. I know you love this man, but you never would have loved him if you had a choice. Maybe it's water under the bridge for you, but it'll never be that way for me."

"It was never any of your business. You shouldn't have even asked him that."

"When a man has vowed to kill my whole family, yes, it's my damn business, Vanessa. If he wants my daughter, he needs to prove he's worthy of her. And that asshole isn't worthy of you at all. His father raped my wife and killed my sister. You think I'm going to let this endless cycle continue with you? My only daughter? The only woman in the world I love more than my damn wife?" His nostrils flared and his shoulders tightened. Slight shakes erupted down his arms, like he wanted to punch the painting on his left. "Every man has a few skeletons in his closet. If he didn't, that would be more alarming. But this man is despicable. His actions are unforgivable. Your affection and lust have blinded you to what's right in front of you. I'm not a man who's blinded by anything—"

"Except hatred," I spat. "Maybe what he did was wrong, but he's not that man anymore. He's grown into someone who does deserve me. He's grown into someone who should love me. When he came home and told me what happened, I said I didn't care what you thought. I said I wasn't going to let my family keep us apart because I couldn't live without him. You know what he said?"

My father was too angry to show vulnerability. Now he stared at me coldly, his eyes shifting back and forth slightly. We'd always been close as I aged. Anytime we fought, it was over something petty. But the second Bones came into my life, the distance between us seemed to get bigger and bigger.

"He said I would regret it later. He said my family means more to me than anything else in this world, and he would never get in the middle of that. He knows what it's like not to have a family, how depressing it is, and he would never want me to understand how that feels…"

Silence.

"You can say what you want about him, but his love

is selfless, true, and real. He would do anything for me…even let me go."

He remained quiet, his green eyes still fierce.

"He's proven himself a million times over, Father. You need to let it go."

"I can let go of a lot of things. I can forget who his father was. I can forget that he's a hitman for a living. I can forget that he captured you with the intent of killing you. But forcing you to sleep with him…I can't forget that. I will never forget it." His chest rose with the deep breath he took, and his nostrils flared again. His anger reached a new peak. "I don't give a shit if he's a saint now. He crossed a line he can never uncross. I will never forgive him for what he did. My decision is final. And you will thank me for it one day."

I took a step back, the distance between us not enough. My father and I would never agree on this matter. I was a grown woman, but his decision somehow dominated mine. If my family didn't mean so much to me, I would storm out of there and run away with Bones. But even when I was livid, the anger was never strong enough to overcast my love. I hated my father in that moment…but I would never hate him more than I loved him. "You should go."

His anger simmered slightly, showing his disappointment.

"I'm not ready to move on. I'm not ready to come over for dinner and be a family again. Right now, I'm devastated. I don't want to pretend nothing happened. I don't want to pretend that everything is fine. I just want to be alone." Instead of waiting for him to walk out, I turned around and drifted away, keeping my back to him so I wouldn't have to see the rage on his face any longer.

My father didn't move, staring at my back in silence.

I didn't want to ask him to leave again, so I stared at the painting on the wall and waited. I had all the patience in the world since I had nothing to live for at the moment. I could wait all day.

Finally, his footsteps tapped against the hardwood floor as he headed to the door. They grew fainter as time passed, and then they disappeared altogether once the door shut behind him.

The gallery turned quiet now that he was gone.

I stared at the painting of Bones in my bed, his chest bare and his face cut out of the frame. My eyes started to well with tears for the hundredth time, but these tears were for a whole new reason. I felt so distant from my father, the man I'd trusted my whole life. He was the kind of man that inspired me, that made me a stronger person. I'd always imagined my husband would be like him, and ironically, I thought he and Bones were a lot alike. But now, he was the reason I was so devastated. He used to protect me from everything, but now he was the very reason I could barely stand on my own two feet.

He was the reason I could barely breathe.

THREE

Crow

I drove out of Florence and into the countryside, one hand on the wheel as I pushed the car to the maximum speed. My brother called me twice, but I rejected his call each time. My eyes looked across the golden fields in front of me, but I didn't care about the beautiful scenery I looked at every day.

All I cared about was my daughter.

My *tesoro*.

My little girl.

I wasn't ignorant to the fact that she was a grown woman. Not only that, but she was exceptionally bright, sassy like her mother, and possessed a hunger for life and adventure. I trusted her instincts because I'd raised her right.

But I couldn't accept the man she loved.

Stubbornness was in my blood, but that wasn't the only reason I didn't accept Griffin.

I hated him.

I hated him so much I almost pulled the trigger. I fantasized about his blood staining the furniture in my office. I pictured the way his eyes would become lifeless once his heart stopped beating. I would give anything to go back in time and kill him before he ever met my daughter.

She deserved better.

She deserved the best.

It killed me to watch her push me away, the man she used to come to for help. But now, she'd turned her back on me, could barely look me in the eye because she was so angry. It broke my heart, to watch my daughter suffer and hate me at the same time.

But I still wouldn't change my mind.

I loved being a father to my two wonderful kids. But this was one of the rare times when it was almost too difficult to bear. She might not understand right now, but I really was doing the best thing for her. She would find the right man to marry, and she would be grateful it wasn't that piece of trash.

When I returned to the house, I didn't tell Button I was home and headed straight to my study on the third floor. It was one of those rare times when I didn't want my wife to console me. I preferred a large glass of aged scotch.

I sat behind my desk, the amber liquid the only company I wanted at that moment. I was an ugly man, bitter and angry. There was so much hatred inside me I didn't know what to do with it. I contemplated hunting Bones down and killing him anyway. I told him to leave my daughter alone and he listened to me, but I wanted to bury him in the ground anyway.

I hated how much pain my daughter was in.

I hated how thin she looked. I hated the blank expression in her eyes. I hated the way life's vigor had been sucked from her body and now she was empty like everyone else in the world.

I'd been watching her for weeks. I watched her make a home in the apartment above the gallery. With pride in my chest, I watched my daughter figure out the wiring in the ceiling to install two chandeliers. I watched her remodel the place entirely on her own, looking up tutorial videos and buying the tools she needed to get the job done. She never asked anyone for help, not even me. Even when she lost the man she loved, she remained independent and strong, knowing she was capable of starting over on her own.

One day, my body would fail me, and I would be buried in the Italian soil beside my parents and sister in the cemetery. Button would be alright because she would have all my wealth to take care of her. She would also have my brother and our son to look after her. But once she was gone, my kids would be on their own.

I needed to know they would be okay.

Vanessa was smart and independent and resourceful. She never gave up, even if the odds were stacked against her. She wasn't afraid to speak her mind, to be a strong woman who didn't care if she seemed bossy. She was capable of taking care of herself. But that wasn't enough for me.

I wanted to know there was a man taking care of her.

I wanted to know he would protect her with his life, provide for her so she could paint for the rest of her life, and he was powerful enough to intimidate anyone from crossing her. I wanted this man to love her as much as I did, to love her the way I loved my wife.

That wasn't Bones.

That man forced my daughter to please him in exchange for not killing her family.

When my hand started to shake with rage, I picked up the glass and threw it across the room. It shattered against the stone fireplace, flying into shards that sprinkled the rug and hardwood floor.

I should kill him.

I should hunt him down with Cane and slice his throat.

I shouldn't have let him walk out of my office without any broken bones.

Footsteps sounded a moment later, and Button stepped inside. In a long blue dress with her hair in a braid over one shoulder, she looked more beautiful than royalty. With fatigue in her eyes from working at the winery all day and not a drop of makeup, she was still a gorgeous woman. Time had changed her appearance, but it couldn't touch her beauty.

She was just as stunning to me as the day I married her.

She shut the door behind her then regarded me with concerned eyes. With fair skin and blue eyes, she was a dream. Her arms crossed over her chest, and she slowly approached the desk.

I'd thrown the glass out of anger, but part of me wondered if I did it to get her attention. I'd come to rely on her to sheathe my rage, to make me see reason when my stubbornness wouldn't allow it.

I didn't look at her, keeping my eyes focused on the cold fireplace.

She rested her fingertips on the top of the open scotch bottle. She stood there quietly, staring at my side profile. My chest rose and fell with my deep breathing, with my fury, and she watched me struggle with my demons.

She picked up the bottle and took a drink, despite the fact that she hated scotch. She wasn't a fan of my drinking habits, but she knew nothing she said would change my love for booze. She accepted me exactly as I was—all the good and the bad. She set the bottle down again and stared at me, waiting for me to meet her look.

I refused to do it.

"Didn't go well?"

My silence was a sufficient answer.

"Give her more time."

"It's been three weeks."

"It's going to take her at least three months."

I sighed under my breath, the sound coming out as a growl. "You've got to be fucking kidding me. That man isn't worth three months of her time."

"It'll take her three months before she *starts* to feel better. For her to really move past this…? At least a year."

I growled again. "I should have killed him. When Conway saw him at the Underground, I should have killed him. He never would have met Vanessa, and this nightmare wouldn't be happening. I didn't protect my family like I promised I would."

Her hand moved to my shoulder, and she dug her fingers into my tight muscles. "Vanessa didn't want to be protected. She loves this man."

"No, she doesn't. She was brainwashed and manipulated."

She massaged her fingers into my shoulder a little longer before she pulled her hand away. "Crow."

I recognized the tone, had listened to it through the decades of our marriage. "What?"

"Look at me."

I kept staring at the fireplace, the cold stones more welcoming than my wife's gaze. I finally turned my head and looked at her, staring into the ocean of disappointment.

"The hypocrisy is baffling." Button never judged me for the man I had been. She never held the past against me. She'd always accepted me for all my darker aspects. It was one of the reasons why I loved her— because she really loved all of me.

"It's not the same. You know it's not."

"It's exactly the same." She propped one hand on her hip. "Crow, you gave me two options. I would either be your prisoner until the day I died, or I could sleep with you in exchange for my freedom."

"But I didn't threaten to kill you or your family."

She rolled her eyes. "You still took my freedom, Crow."

"It's not like you had any other place to go."

Her eyes narrowed immediately, showing their outrage and pain at the same time.

I immediately regretted what I'd said. "That came out wrong."

"Yes," she said coldly. "It did."

"Vanessa has a family that loves her. She has a father who would die for her. I'm not letting her settle for anything less than the best. I'm not giving her away to a monster that doesn't deserve her."

"And you think you don't deserve me?" she challenged.

I'd been married to her for thirty years, had committed my life to loving her and protecting her, but none of that could make up for what I did. "No. I'll never deserve you, Button."

She cocked her head to the side slightly, her eyes softening.

"You deserved a man much better than me." I looked at the fireplace again, remembering the night she gave herself to me. I told her she could be free if she earned her freedom. And in the end, she never did. She was mine the second she came into my possession.

"Even if that's true, I've never wanted anyone else, Crow."

I still couldn't look at her. "Vanessa never would have loved him if he didn't force her."

"And I may never have loved you either. But I still wouldn't change anything."

It didn't matter how similar the situations were. I would never view the circumstances differently. "Our daughter deserves a better love story. She deserves respect. I want a man who falls to his knees for her. I want a man who will bend over backward for her."

"Maybe that's not what she's looking for."

"Too bad. It's what she deserves."

She crossed her arms over her chest. "I don't need to tell you this, Crow. But our daughter has been a grown woman for a long time—"

"I don't want to talk about this." I knew exactly what she was going to say. I never thought about my daughter's personal life. It was a subject I never touched, letting Button handle it exclusively. I was so protective of Vanessa that it was a subject I couldn't discuss with an open mind. If I could have gotten away with it, I would have forced her into an arranged marriage with a man of my choice, and that would be the end of the discussion.

She sighed under her breath. "Our daughter is very

resourceful. If she really didn't want to be in that situation, she would have gotten out of it. When you and I—"

"I said, I don't want to talk about this. Don't make me repeat myself." I grabbed the bottle and took a long drink, letting the booze burn my throat all the way down to my stomach. "You don't agree with my decision?"

Button was quiet for a long time, pondering my question in silence. When she finally answered, her voice was gentle. "Does it matter? My opinion won't change yours."

"No, it won't. But I want to know anyway."

"I don't like the pretense of their relationship. I don't even like him…because of his father. But I really believe they love each other."

I believed it too. I saw the way he looked at her, saw the way she looked at him. "She'll love someone else. In time, she will."

"I know. But I don't think she'll ever love anyone the way she loved him. If I had to move on from you… I certainly wouldn't have forgotten about you."

Her life would have been better off if she had. Most of our relationship had been spent in peace and quiet, but it hadn't always been that way. There were times when we thought we wouldn't survive. "This is the best decision for all of us. He doesn't deserve her, and the Barsettis will never look past the crimes that have damaged this family. I will never welcome a man who forced my daughter into submission. I don't care if he loves her. I don't care if he's rich or powerful. I only want a man who will love and respect my daughter—and he's not that man."

FOUR

Conway

_____

I felt the Italian material in my hands, a fabric that was so soft against my fingertips it felt like silk. But it had the ideal elasticity to stretch in all the necessary ways. It would be perfect for my next piece, a maternity ensemble that would look great on Muse. Her pregnancy had aroused me in ways I couldn't explain, and now the lingerie I made for work was used for personal reasons.

After measuring the material, I cut it in the precise place.

A knock sounded on the door before Muse walked inside. She wore a green dress that was loose around her stomach. Her pregnancy had swollen her belly, making her stomach distended and round. She'd gained some weight everywhere, but her stomach was the most affected. "Are you busy right now?"

I put down the scissors and measuring tape, ignoring her question because it was stupid. I was never too busy for her. Never had been and never would be. I rose from the stool and moved my hand to her belly, feeling the curve underneath my hand. I could feel our baby inside her, feel it kick in the middle of the night when she was asleep. My eyes lifted to her face, and I saw the most beautiful woman I'd ever laid eyes on, the woman who would become my wife. "Everything alright?" I kept my hand on her stomach, waiting for a kick.

"Nothing's wrong," she said. "But I just put on my wedding dress, and it doesn't fit…" Her eyes fell in sadness, like that was something to be embarrassed about. "The baby is making me bigger at a much quicker pace now."

"Good. It's getting big and healthy." I lifted up her dress so I could press my palm against her bare skin. Her belly was firm and warm, the curvature of her stomach sexy. I'd never had a thing for pregnant women, but when it came to mine, she made me hard instantly.

Her eyes held her sadness. "Yes, I'm happy about that. But…" She tilted her head down. "Never mind."

My fingers moved under her chin, and I lifted her head. "Tell me."

Her eyes were still hesitant, subtly fighting me. "I'm getting so big that I'll never look good in a wedding dress."

"You look good naked, so don't worry about it."

She hit my arm playfully. "I'm being serious. I don't want to be insensitive to Vanessa, but I just hit my seventh month. If I wait any longer, I won't be able to wear heels. And I want to be married before the baby comes…"

My mother told me what had happened with my father and Bones. I'd be lying if I said I wasn't relieved. I respected my father for making the right decision even though it made Vanessa angry. My sister deserved a good man, not an enemy to the Barsetti line. "What do you want to do?"

"I want to get married…"

My hands went to her lower back, feeling the sharp curve in her spine from the weight of her stomach. "Then we'll get married." My eyes looked into her blue ones, seeing the emotions running deep.

"What about Vanessa?"

"Don't worry about her. She'll be happy for us."

"I don't know…she just lost the man she loves. She doesn't want to watch anyone get married."

"We're family. It'll make her happy."

"I feel selfish for even thinking about it…"

I lowered my face so I could rest my forehead against hers. I spent every waking moment with this woman, and the time we spent preparing for the baby made me love her in a new way. I felt like we were a family even though we weren't married yet, even though we didn't have a child yet. It was hard to believe I was ever a jerk to her in the past. "You aren't being selfish, Muse. The world doesn't stop because of Vanessa."

"I want to go to Florence and see her. Make sure she's okay with it."

I loved my sister, but I didn't need her approval for anything. "That's unnecessary."

"I want to check on her anyway. Then maybe we could do the ceremony at your parents' place. I'll just have to get my dress let out…"

"You know I can do that for you."

"You aren't supposed to see the dress, remember?"

"Then Lars can do it."

"No, he's too old for that."

"Trust me, he enjoys it," I said. "Doing stuff for the family keeps him happy. So, you want to do this?"

She nodded. "I want to be Mrs. Barsetti."

Hearing her call herself that only made me want

her more. I couldn't wait to hear people call her that, to refer to her as my wife. She wore my last name just as well as she wore my lingerie. "I do too."

ACCORDING TO MY FATHER, Vanessa had her own gallery in Florence. It was in the center of town, right next door to a bakery. Her apartment was above the gallery, a two-bedroom space my father approved of. A cobblestone road was in front of it, the sidewalk packed with motorbikes. People were walking down the side-walks, their coffees and shopping bags in hand. Florence was different from Milan because it was much smaller, packed with antique shops and small restaurants.

Muse seemed to love it as much as Milan. "I like it here."

"It's the capital of Tuscany." I parked on the side of the road, squeezing in between two small cars. My father told me this was where Vanessa had been spending her time. She was still just as devastated as she was a month ago, never leaving her gallery or the apartment upstairs. She kept to herself, dealing with her misery in solitude. I didn't just come here because Muse wanted to check in on my sister.

I was worried about her too.

She'd made her feelings for Griffin very clear, that she loved him in a way she would never love anyone else. I could hear the sincerity in her voice when she spoke, the way it cracked a little when there was so much emotion in her throat. I recognize the love in her eyes, because it was the same love that was in mine.

I was happy Griffin was gone, but I was sad my sister was in so much pain.

Muse and I entered the gallery, and fortunately, no one else was inside. The walls were covered with paint-ings, and I wasn't surprised that most of them contained the man she loved. There was one image in particular that was too uncomfortable for me to look at. It showed him in her bed, shirtless with the sheets around his waist. I didn't like to picture Vanessa with men, even though I wasn't ignorant to the fact that she was a grown woman. It made me sick to my stomach.

Muse glanced at all the paintings, and instead of being disgusted by the one I hated, she actually smiled when she looked at it.

I grabbed her arm and gently pulled her away, not wanting my fiancée to look at Bones shirtless. The guy might be an enemy to my family, but there was no denying he was a handsome man.

Vanessa came around the corner, wearing jeans and

a white V-neck. Her dark hair was pulled back in a loose bun, and there was no denying she'd lost several inches around her waist. She was already thin to begin with, and she didn't need to lose any weight. The scar from the gunshot was still visible on her left arm. Her olive skin contrasted against the white shirt she wore. It took her a moment to recognize us because it seemed like she was deep in thought. "Sapphire? Conway?" She blinked a few times before she finally allowed a smile to creep onto her lips. "What are you guys doing here?"

"Wanted to see your new gallery," Muse said. "And it looks amazing. You did a great job with it." Muse moved in and hugged her, turning slightly to the side to get her stomach out of the way. She held Vanessa for a while, supporting her friend with a warm embrace.

Vanessa hugged her back and let the embrace linger, clinging to it like it was exactly what she needed.

I looked away, feeling my sister's sadness sink into my bones.

"How are you doing?" Muse asked quietly.

Vanessa didn't answer.

Muse pulled away and rubbed my sister's back, her lips pressed tightly together and her eyes emotional. When I'd pushed Muse away, she went to New York and tried to start over without me. She knew exactly how Vanessa felt, losing the man she loved. "Your paintings are beautiful."

"Thanks, Sapphire," Vanessa said, her words hollow like a rotted tree trunk. She turned her gaze to me next, her eyes lacking the usual light they held. She would normally greet me with a sassy comment or insult me in a playful manner. But now her social skills seemed to be nonexistent. She didn't know how to interact with people.

I hated seeing my strong sister so crushed.

I moved into her and wrapped my arms around her, holding her in a rare gesture of affection. We hardly ever touched, but whenever she was struggling, the protective side of me emerged. I wanted her to be happy. I wanted her to have everything she wanted. When that didn't happen, it made me feel the same pain she felt. I held her against my chest and rested my chin on her head, my hand running down her back. I felt her breathe against me, doing her best to keep her emotions intact. "I'm sorry."

She turned her cheek against my chest, letting me hold her for the longest period in history. She breathed harder, like she was restraining the tears that burned in her eyes. Her arms remained around my waist, and she accepted the comfort that I gave her.

Muse watched us, her eyes watering slightly.

When Knuckles took my sister away, I was afraid I would never get her back. I was scared to lose someone I loved, and it made me realize just how much she meant to me. Now, I was even more convinced of my unconditional love because I felt so much pain listening to her try not to cry. "You'll get through it, Vanessa."

I must have said the wrong thing because she pulled away. "You guys didn't have to come by and check on me…even though I appreciate it."

"We wanted to see you." Muse wrapped her arm around Vanessa's waist. "We're really excited for your gallery. And you have to show us your apartment. Your father mentioned that it was nice."

"He's never seen my apartment," she whispered.

That's what she thought. "Give us a tour, then we'll grab something to eat."

"I'm not hungry," she said automatically.

"Maybe when we walk into a restaurant, it'll get your appetite going," Muse said. "That's what usually happens to me…"

Vanessa gave us a tour of the gallery before she took us upstairs to her apartment. Most of the furniture was the stuff from Milan, and she had a few extra pieces that must have come with it. I spotted the painting on the wall, another one of Bones. This time, it was of him looking across a cold lake in the middle of winter. It showed his broad shoulders and his thick arms but not his face.

"It looks really nice." Muse did her best to keep Vanessa in a good mood by being complimentary. She never addressed Bones or the horrible breakup Vanessa was struggling through. "And your commute to work is nice," she teased.

Vanessa cracked a smile, but it was fake. "Thanks. You guys want some wine?"

"I'll take some," I answered. "Just water for Sapphire."

"Of course," Vanessa said, cringing at her ignorance. "I wasn't thinking…"

"It's okay," Muse said. "Don't worry about it."

Vanessa walked into the kitchen and gathered the glasses and water.

I helped Muse onto the couch before I sat beside her.

"She's such a wreck…" Muse whispered so only I could hear.

"Yeah…" It was worse than I'd thought.

"I feel so bad for her."

"I do too."

"I wish there was something we could do."

"I think being here is all we can do." Vanessa would have to get through this on her own. Right now, it seemed like the end of the world, but there was nothing she couldn't overcome. She was much stronger than she realized.

Vanessa returned a moment later with a bottle of wine, a few glasses, and some French bread with olive oil.

I was surprised she had any food on hand since she seemed to have lost so much weight in a short amount of time. Muse and I sat on the other couch and faced Vanessa, seeing the heartbroken look in her eyes.

She didn't bother hiding it. There was a distinct hollowness in her eyes, an emptiness that couldn't be filled without the passage of time. Her skin seemed sunken in, like she was dehydrated. Her clothes didn't fit her quite the same, baggy around the arms and stomach.

I wanted to say something to get the conversation moving, but seeing my sister so distraught erased my train of thought. I'd never seen her be anything but strong. In the face of serious danger, she had the nerve to laugh. She was younger than me, but I admired her in a lot of ways. She possessed Mama's beauty but Father's hardness. Our father let me get away with more things than her simply because I was a man. He was a million times harder on her, and not just when it came to boys and dating. When he taught her to use a gun, she was a natural, but nothing was ever good enough. He trained her to become a killing machine. When it came to me, he didn't think I needed as much attention.

Vanessa crossed her legs and poured two glasses of wine. "So…what's new with you guys? How's the baby?"

Muse absentmindedly rubbed her stomach. "Baby is great. It's been kicking a lot lately…mainly when I'm sleeping."

The corner of Vanessa's mouth rose in a smile. "Perfect timing, huh?"

"Yeah," Muse said with a chuckle. "But I've been sleeping in late to catch up on the restless nights."

Vanessa shifted her gaze to me. "And you don't have to suffer at all…nice being a father."

I didn't have to deal with morning sickness, sleep loss, or discomfort. I got to enjoy all the benefits, like making love to Muse and getting off on her pregnant belly. Hottest thing in the world. I thought I was only attracted to thin models who could rock the runway in heels, but I found my pregnant and waddling fiancée to be the sexiest thing I've ever seen. "Pretty much."

"Got any names yet?" Vanessa was cooperative in the conversation, smiling when she was supposed to, but the hint of sadness in her eyes could never be erased.

"No, not yet," Muse said. "We think we're going to stick to names that start with a C, though. Seems to be a Barsetti tradition."

Vanessa shook her head. "You don't need to stick to tradition. The Barsetti last name is tradition enough."

"We haven't put a lot of thought into the name," I said. "I've been more concerned about the baby getting here and being healthy. That's all I care about." My eyes went to Muse's swollen stomach that stretched her dress. Inside was the little person who would become my whole world. They already were my whole world.

"The baby will be healthy," Vanessa said with certainty. "And they'll be wonderful and beautiful. Don't worry about it." Her eyes turned to Muse's stomach. "I'm very excited to be an aunt, and not just to turn them against you."

I let her taunt slide. "You'll be a great aunt."

Muse smiled. "Yes, you will be."

Vanessa's smile slowly faded away, like a different thought was entering her brain. It must have been something about Bones, because that look of depression returned. "Are you ever getting married?"

"Actually, we were thinking about doing it soon,"

Muse said. "I'm getting so big, and I know once the baby gets here, we'll be too busy and tired…"

"You should do it," Vanessa said. "Enjoy being married for a few months before your family grows."

I knew Vanessa wouldn't be offended about us tying the knot. She'd never been a self-absorbed person, even in her darkest hour.

"We were thinking about doing it on Saturday, actually…" Muse lowered her hand from her stomach. "My dress needs to be let out a little bit, but that shouldn't take too long. We wanted to do something small, just a dinner at the house."

"That sounds like a great idea." Vanessa raised her glass of wine. "I'm in."

"You're sure?" Muse asked uncertainly.

"Of course." Vanessa took a drink. "Why wouldn't I be? I'm excited to have a sister. It's much better than having a brother."

Muse smiled. "I just wanted to make sure."

Vanessa's smile faded away when she understood the reason Muse was concerned. She connected the dots slowly, and then reality hit her. "If you're worried about me because of what happened with…" She couldn't say his name. She grimaced, like the formation of the words on her tongue somehow stung her. "Don't be. I'm very happy for both of you. This is a really exciting time in your lives, and I'm very happy to share it with you."

———

WHEN WE TOLD my parents about the wedding, they were both excited. Father was a little different, obviously upset over his shaky relationship with Vanessa. Muse made the plans with my mom, and together with Lars, they planned the dinner and the decorations. Lars agreed to adjust her dress so it would fit her just right, and I was left to wait around until the big day.

That was fine with me. I didn't care about planning a wedding. All I cared about was the woman who wanted to be my wife. Her dress would be beautiful, but it would be more beautiful on the bedroom floor.

I was working on my laptop in my old bedroom, the one Muse and I were using for the time being. For the actual wedding night, I would take her somewhere else. It would be strange to spend our honeymoon in my parents' house. I would have flown Muse off to a beautiful place, but since she was so late in her pregnancy, getting her around was nearly impossible.

A knock sounded on the door. "Can I come in?" Father's deep voice penetrated the solid wood of the door.

"You never used to ask when I was a kid."

He opened the door, a slight grin on his face. "You didn't have any rights as a kid." His ripped arms stretched the sleeves of his t-shirt. He carried himself like a king, even when no one was watching. He lowered himself into the chair across the room and leaned back, resting one ankle on the opposite knee. He seemed happy I was there, sharing the house with him and my mother once again, but there was a definite sadness in his eyes.

I knew the cause of his sorrow. "She'll come around."

He lifted his gaze and met mine. Heartbeats passed, but he didn't blink. It was strange to see him without a glass in his hand. Mama probably cut him off. I'd never seen my father drunk, but then again, maybe he was always drunk and I've never seen him sober. "You think so?"

I gave a slight nod. "She's the strongest woman I know…but don't tell her I said that."

My father would normally crack a smile, but this time, he didn't. "She is."

"She just needs more time."

"How was she when you saw her?"

She looked like a ghost. Her olive skin wasn't as dark as it usually was. She didn't wear makeup, and her eyes didn't shine with that inner brightness. "Defeated. But her good qualities are still there. She seemed genuinely happy that Muse and I…I mean Sapphire… are getting married. The old Vanessa is still in there… just buried deep under her sorrow." I shut my laptop and gave my father my full attention.

"That's what you call her?" he asked. "Muse?"

I gave a slight nod.

The corner of his mouth rose in a smile before it fell down again. "I can't remember the last time I addressed your mother by her first name. Sometimes I forget what it is."

"Same here."

We sat in silence for a while, my father's hands coming together in his lap. His gaze moved to the open window, the view of the vineyards endless. He was always composed and rigid, but right now, he seemed particularly stiff. "It was a hard decision. It was hard because I knew how much it would hurt her. I know she loves him…and I think he loves her. But I had to do the right thing. I'm not going to be around forever, and I want to die peacefully, to know my only daughter is with a man who will do a better job taking care of her than I ever did. That's all I want. Maybe it's selfish… but it's what I need."

I wasn't a father just yet, but I felt the same way

about my baby. Whether it was a boy or a girl, it didn't matter. It would be nice to know they had someone else to take care of them if I weren't around. "What changed your mind?"

My father's gaze turned back to me, and he held my look for a long time. After a slight shake of his head, he cleared his throat. "Doesn't matter. He's not right for her."

I knew he was hiding something from me, but I didn't press him on it. "I think you made the right decision. When our hatred runs so deep, it's unlikely the Barsettis will ever accept someone like him. Maybe Vanessa loves him, but she can love someone else."

My father closed his eyes for a brief moment and nodded. "I hope so."

"But I do hate her misery. I've never seen her this low."

"Neither have I. I stopped by her gallery to see her last week…she can barely look at me." He took a deep breath, his features tightening in obvious pain. "I know I need to be patient, but having my only daughter hate me is killing me. I can barely sleep." His eyes shifted away, the pain coating his entire expression.

My father was such a strong man that I'd never pitied him. He never allowed anything to bother him. If he carried any pain, he hid it from everyone. But now his sorrow was so deep he couldn't hide it. He wore it on his sleeve, showed it in his face. "She doesn't hate you, Father. I know she doesn't."

He wouldn't look at me.

"If she did, she wouldn't still be here. She would have run off with him and turned her back on all of us. But she didn't. We're the most important thing in the world to her. She needed your approval to be with him, and when she didn't get it, she let him go. She loves you more than she'll ever love a man."

He turned his gaze back on me, the emotion burning in his eyes. "That's nice of you to say, son."

"It's the truth. Be patient, she'll come around."

"I've never been a patient man…but I suppose I'll have to learn to be one."

———

"YOU'RE GETTING MARRIED TOMORROW." Carter sat across from me at the picnic table on the grass. Mama and Muse were working on the decorations for outside, placing the colorful flowers in the gazebo where we would get married. "We've got to hit the town tonight. It's your last night as a bachelor, so we've got to make it count."

"I haven't been a bachelor for a long time."

"You may have been whipped for a long time, but you have been a bachelor." Carter drank his beer and watched everyone work in the yard. "Come on, we'll take our fathers and hit a strip club."

I cocked an eyebrow. "You want to take our fathers to a strip club?"

"Why not?" he asked. "It's a bachelor party."

"They're whipped even more than I am. No way they'd set foot in that kind of place." My father was too rigid for something like that. I'd never even seen him glance at another woman. He seemed to only have eyes for my mother.

"They're men just like us. I'm sure they'd come."

"Carter, we aren't going to a strip club."

"Why the hell not?" he demanded. "It's one time, one night. Sapphire doesn't seem like a woman that would care."

She wouldn't care. She knew I worked with models all day, every day. I designed sex clothes for them to wear so men would fantasize about fucking them. It made them buy my lingerie for their women at home. "I don't care that she doesn't care. I'm the one who cares."

He rolled his eyes and took a drink. "When did you get so lame?"

"I'm gonna be a father in a few months, in case you've forgotten."

"So that means you need to be boring?" he demanded. "Pussy shit?"

"You want me to slam your face into the table?" I countered. "I don't mind going out for a drink or two, but I don't want to watch women get naked. When you find the right woman, you'll understand where I'm coming from."

"I've found a lot of *right* women," he said. "But I'll never understand your point of view."

"Because they aren't the one."

Carter dropped the hostility. "So, we'll head to Florence for a drink?"

"That works for me. While we're there, I think we should invite Vanessa."

Carter looked even more skeptical than before. "Your sister? You want to invite your sister to your bachelor party?"

"It's not a bachelor party. And yes, I think it would be good to get her out of the house."

"Jesus, that sounds terrible. That means Carmen will have to come."

"Not a bad idea."

Carter grimaced, like he'd just taken a bite of

spoiled food. "This is how you want to spend your last night as a single man?"

I hadn't felt single in a long time. "I saw Vanessa last week, and she looked awful. She's not staying at the house for the wedding because she's still avoiding Father. She could use the company. I'm not happy about it either…but that's what families do."

Carter didn't argue, understanding my point immediately. Family was important to both of us. It was something we both agreed on without saying a word. He sighed with disappointment but didn't express his anger with words. "Alright. Let's do it."

———

CARMEN AND VANESSA sat across from us at the table in the bar. Carmen was dressed up in a blue dress with her hair big and curled. She wore a lot of makeup, and she was attracting attention with every passing second.

Vanessa was of the opposite nature. In jeans and a t-shirt, she was dressed too casually for the bar. The only reason she got inside was because she was still pretty no matter how sad she looked. She didn't wear makeup, and her hair was pulled back in the same bun she'd worn the other day.

Carter wasn't happy about the girls tagging along, but he didn't make a fuss about it. He enjoyed his beer, his eyes scanning the room for a possible woman to take home. Carter went through women with the same efficiency I used to possess. He had good looks, lots of money, and he had the kind of confidence women were innately attracted to. It was surprising that I'd settled down, but the possibility of that happening to Carter was nonexistent.

He would never be a one-woman kind of guy.

Carmen spotted a man across the room, her eyes following him as he carried his beer from the bar to the table where his friends were waiting. "He's cute."

Vanessa drank her scotch, her eyes cast downward. "Go talk to him."

"I pointed him out for you." Carmen tucked her dark hair behind her ear, her eyelashes luscious and thick. Carmen had the same exotic look that Vanessa had, but she possessed her mother's features a little more. As a result, she was a very beautiful woman… much to my uncle's annoyance.

"Thanks." Vanessa still didn't look, obviously not interested in anyone in that bar. "So, what next?"

"What do you mean?" Carter asked.

"Are we going to a strip club next?" Carmen asked.

"Or a club in general?" Vanessa asked.

"We're keeping it quiet tonight." Having a drink with my family was enough of an adventure. I kept Muse in mind, constantly worrying if she was doing okay. My parents were there if she needed something, but the bigger her belly became, the more I worried.

"Seriously?" Vanessa asked, her eyebrow raised.

"You've got to be kidding me," Carmen said, appalled.

"What?" Carter asked incredulously. "You guys *want* to go to a strip club?"

"Not necessarily," Vanessa said. "But this is a bachelor party, right?"

"Not really," I said. "We're just getting a drink and enjoying each other's company."

"Enjoying each other's company?" Vanessa asked. "You never enjoy my company."

"Very good point," Carmen said, her fingers wrapped around her beer. "Carter never enjoys mine."

"I'm not interested in strippers. I'm not interested in anything crazy." I had a famous face, and I hated being recognized everywhere I went. I was usually recognized by women, and most of the time they tried to make a move. I used to live for those moments, to have beautiful women show interest, but now my life was different. I'd never wanted to settle down because I didn't want to be boring, to stop living life on the town. But that happened anyway, and I didn't regret it.

"So, you are boring," Vanessa noted.

I would normally put her down in some way, but since she was going through a hard time, I let it slide. Until she was better, I would keep my mouth shut. "I'm a committed man."

"Boring," Carmen said. "When I get married, I'm hitting the strip club. I'm gonna dance on the bar and give my panties to some stranger."

Carter cringed. "Anyway…"

Vanessa turned quiet, the sadness entering her eyes.

Carmen realized what she'd said and wore a look of regret. "I just meant——"

"Don't walk on eggshells around me," Vanessa said gently. "Really, it's fine. I'm going to be this way for a long time, but you shouldn't have to watch everything you say to avoid offending me. Heartbreak is a complicated thing…I've never felt this way before. Everything reminds me of him, so I can never really escape this pain. Even when I sleep, he's there…" Her eyes drifted down to her scotch. She gripped the glass tightly, the only person there who'd gone straight for the hard liquor.

"I'm sorry," Carmen whispered. "I wish there were something I could do…"

Vanessa rubbed her back. "You're already doing something."

"You know, maybe you should start seeing someone," Carmen said. "They say the quickest way to get over someone is to get under someone else…"

I would normally grimace or tell them to drop the subject, but I bit my tongue. Vanessa had to put up with my relationship with Muse since they were friends, so I should be quiet and not say anything.

"I'm not interested in that," Vanessa said, her eyes heavy. "I can't even picture myself with someone else. I'm not there. I won't be there for a long time."

Carmen gave a slight nod. "I understand. Griffin was really hot."

"It was more than that," Vanessa said. "It was deeper than that."

My sister's sadness bothered me, and I wished it would end. I missed her outgoing personality, her fearless ways. I knew this relationship had changed her forever. She would never be quite the same. But I still didn't want Bones back in our lives. "Vanessa."

My sister turned toward me, displaying features that were similar to my own. She looked more like Mama, and I looked more like Father, but it was obvious we were related. "Yeah?"

"How about you stay at the house tonight?" I knew

it would make both of my parents happy, particularly my father. Vanessa used to love staying at her childhood home every chance she got, but all of that changed overnight.

Vanessa stared at me, but her expression didn't change, still full of heavy sorrow. "I don't want to." She said it simply and without a drop of emotion. She held my gaze before she turned back to her scotch.

I kept looking at her, surprised she'd given such a deadpan response. "It would mean a lot to Father if you did."

"I'm not ready to pretend everything is okay, Conway." She spoke directly to me while our cousins listened to every single word. They were silent, blending into the background while music played over-head. "Because everything is not okay. I'm happy for both of you, and I'm excited to see my brother get married. Sapphire is a wonderful person, and you're very lucky to have each other. I'm excited to call her my sister. But my issues with Father are separate, and I can't dwell on it tomorrow. But no, I'm not going to sleep over and pretend everything is okay. Father made the wrong decision."

Carter shifted his gaze back and forth between us, the tension palpable.

Carmen cleared her throat, twirling a strand of hair at the same time.

Our cousins were aware of the situation, but the intensity of our discussion was obviously heavy for the lighthearted evening. "Guys, could you give us a minute?"

"Sure thing." Carter couldn't wait to get away from the table. He headed to the bar, taking his drink with him. Carmen joined him, the two of them sitting together. They were distant with one another, so it was obvious they weren't a couple.

Vanessa kept staring at me. "Let's not talk about this right now."

"Too late. It's happening." I drank my beer then returned the heavy glass to the table. "I know you're upset, but Father did the right thing. He's protecting you. I don't have a son or a daughter yet, but I've been preparing for it since the day Sapphire told me she was pregnant. So I understand how he feels. I want the best for my little one. Vanessa, Griffin is not the best."

"I'm not looking for the best. He's the man I fell in love with. It's not like I have a choice of who I love. That's not how it works. If you ever had a choice, you never would have fallen in love with Sapphire in the first place."

She had me there. "You will meet someone better,

Vanessa."

"But that doesn't mean I'll love him better. I've been with plenty of other guys—"

"I don't want to hear about that." In my fantasy world, my sister never hooked up with guys. She was a nun who painted.

She rolled her eyes. "Get over it, Conway. I'm a grown woman who can do whatever she wants. Your immaturity is completely sexist. You can sleep with every woman in Italy and nobody gives a damn, but with me, there's a double standard. It's bullshit."

"I'm not sexist. I just don't want to hear about your personal life. I don't talk about mine."

"Yes, you do," she argued. "You make comments here and there. Your promiscuity has never been subtle, Conway. Mama and Father have never cared, and I've never cared. But when it comes to me, everything is different. Sapphire was being hunted by a psychopath that kidnapped and almost killed me, but Mama and Father never even raised an eyebrow at her. She's been far more dangerous than Griffin has ever been. It's bull-shit—and you know it."

We'd had this conversation before, and I couldn't deny the stark differences between our relationships. "Sapphire has never been an enemy to this family. She's an innocent woman who would never hurt anyone."

"Griffin would never hurt me or any of you."

"Except when he wanted to murder us all," I snapped. "I've got a wife and a kid to look after now. It gives me peace of mind knowing I don't have to worry about Griffin anymore. I understand that you're angry, but Father made the right decision. It was really hard for him, Vanessa. I've never seen him so low. You're all he thinks about. He thinks you hate him."

"I told him I didn't."

"That's not enough to convince him. Show it."

She crossed her arms over her chest and looked away. "Did Father tell you why he changed his mind?"

"No."

She finished her scotch and turned back to me.

"Are you going to tell me why?"

"It'll make you uncomfortable."

"Then don't tell me."

We sat in silence for a while, quiet conversations filling the bar. Carmen and Carter kept talking over at the counter.

She spoke again. "Father asked Griffin something he never should have asked. He pried into my intimate relationship when it was none of his business. Griffin gave him an answer he didn't want to hear, so Father pulled a gun on him. It was unfair. We'd spent the last two months trying to get our parents to see the man I love for who he is now. And then information from the past came up, and it was like the last two months never happened. It was unfair—completely unfair."

I wasn't sure what secret she was hiding, but it made me think of the skeletons in my own closet. When I met Muse, I wasn't good to her. I demanded sex from her, took her virginity, and kept her as a slave. The only reason I started to treat her as a person was when she demanded for me to. I wasn't a saint by any measure, but I'd never killed anyone or vowed revenge on someone's family. "You picked the worst possible man to love, Vanessa. Mama and Father have been through a lot, and you chose the one person they can't tolerate. With all the men out there, you come home with the only man Father can't stand. You're putting all the blame on him, but you didn't give him much to work with. What did you expect him to do? He did his best, Vanessa. He's always done his best for both of us. You're being a brat, you know that?"

Her eyes filled with hatred. "How would you feel if Father took Sapphire away?"

"I never would have loved a woman who wanted to kill my family."

"You say that now, but you don't know. Trust me, I tried not to fall in love with Griffin. When he told me he loved me, I took off. But it was impossible, Conway.

It was just as impossible as it was for you not to love Sapphire."

"Even so, you aren't giving Father the respect and compassion he deserves. We're both damn lucky that we have a family. Sapphire has no one. You have a father who's willing to protect you even if that means you hate him. Be grateful."

Her eyes flashed like she wanted to sink her nails into my throat. "I never said I hated Father. Obviously, I don't. I've never taken my family for granted. If I did, Griffin wouldn't be gone. So stop putting words in my mouth. I'm not trying to hurt Father, but I can't say I agree with him. He's hypocritical."

"He's just looking after you, Vanessa."

"I'm a grown-ass woman who doesn't need someone to look after me."

"If you think Griffin is a good guy, then you obviously do."

Her eyes narrowed even further. "He's gone, Con. There's no reason to continue to tear me down about it. If you think he's a bad man, you should take a look in the mirror."

"What the hell is that supposed to mean?"

"Sapphire told me everything—the truth about your relationship."

Immediately, the adrenaline flooded my system. My

blood boiled, and my veins burned from the heat. Father knew my secret, but that was different. I never wanted my mother and sister to know what I'd done.

She cocked her head slightly. "You kept her as a prisoner, forced her to please you, and never treated her like a real human being. So sit there and tell me how you're any better than Griffin."

I kept my mouth shut because I didn't have an answer.

"Tell me," she pressed. "What's the difference between you? Because I don't see a damn thing."

"For starters, I never tried to kill Sapphire."

Her eyes narrowed. "But forcing her into a life of sexual servitude is any better?"

"It wasn't like that—"

"That's how she made it sound. Fortunately, she was attracted to you and fell in love with you. And she didn't have a penny to her name and had nowhere to go. You had more power over her, and you took advantage of it. Don't pretend otherwise, Conway. Griffin has always been honest about who he is, and I respect him for it. In that regard, he is better than you. He'll say the truth even if he's hated for it. That's a man, Conway."

My sister had pissed me off a lot while growing up, but she'd never said anything so insulting to me. "Don't compare me to him."

"Then don't judge him unfairly."

My hand shook under the table because I wanted to pick up my chair and slam it onto the floor. Even if my sister was right, I didn't appreciate the unfair sentence she'd just given me. "Maybe I don't tell you every little detail because it's none of your business."

"Yet, my relationship with Griffin has been every-one's business."

"It's different. He—"

"It's not different. Father didn't give a damn how you treated Sapphire, even though it was morally wrong on so many levels. But with Bones, it's a completely different perception. It's sexist. Fundamen-tally sexist."

"It's not sexist. You're the victim in this situation."

"I'm *not* a victim," she hissed. "I was loved and protected by the strongest man on this planet. He worshiped the ground I walked on. Before he left, he bought me a gallery, an apartment, and a car. I've never been happier than I've been with him. No, I wasn't a victim. Far from it." She pushed her chair back and stood up, dismissing the conversation once it reached its peak. She turned around and stormed off without saying another word.

And I didn't try to get her to stay.

FIVE

Vanessa

I couldn't sleep that night.

Even though everything I said was right, I felt guilty for talking to my brother that way.

Underneath his judgments and scrutiny, there was love.

Love was always there.

I sat up in bed, my back against the headboard. The sheets were always chilly because Bones wasn't there to keep them warm. Spring was quickly turning into summer, but the heat still didn't chase the cold away.

Nothing but Bones could chase the cold away.

It'd been a month since he left, and while I'd stopped crying all the time, I was still just as devastated. It was like he'd just left, just gave me our final kiss. His painting kept me company but also made me heart-broken at the same time.

But I could never take it down.

I felt his presence everywhere, especially in my heart. I dreamed of his kiss, of his large body on top of mine. Sometimes I dreamed of us staring at each other, his intense blue eyes looking into mine with possession. That man was embedded so deeply into my heart that the bruise would be there forever.

Another man could never erase him. There would always be a trace there, always be a scar there.

I wondered if this pain would ever end. I couldn't even look at another man because it felt wrong. A man made a pass at me at the bakery the other day, and he was tall and handsome, but I still didn't care.

He wasn't Bones.

I couldn't picture myself making love to someone else, kissing someone else. Even if I did, there would only be one man on my mind. I would close my eyes and pretend it was him instead of the man inside me.

I was just as in love with him as I'd always been.

I sat in the darkness and wondered what he was doing. Where was he? Was he awake at that very moment thinking of me? Had he been with someone else yet? Was he taking this breakup much better than I was?

Did he still love me?

Sometimes I expected to see him across the street from my gallery, watching over me like he always did. But he was never there. At nighttime, I looked out the window and expected his truck to be parked across the street. But he was never there.

There was no reason to protect me anymore. I didn't need to be protected anymore, not when my father was watching me just as intently as he used to. There was no danger surrounding me, not when I lived a quiet life painting.

Bones had no reason to check on me.

I grabbed my phone off the nightstand and stared at the bright screen in the darkness. I'd been tempted to call him so many times, but never as tempted as I was in that moment. Instead of missing him less as time passed, I seemed to miss him more.

I just wanted to hear his voice.

I didn't know what we would talk about. I didn't want to know how he was spending his nights, and he didn't want to know how miserable I was. The conversation would bring us nothing but pain.

I shouldn't call.

My hand shook as I held the phone. My finger ached to pull up his number and make the call. My emotions were erratic, but my logic was somehow stronger. I put the phone back on the nightstand.

But I didn't go to sleep.

I ARRIVED at the house early the next morning, wearing a nice dress that I had to have taken in because it was too big. Father wasn't on my mind because I was thinking about Conway. I didn't like the way we'd left things last night. I had to make it right, even if he was wrong.

I walked into the house and ran into my mother first.

Mama stopped in the entryway, and her smile faded away almost instantly. Her eyes suddenly reflected the sorrow in my heart. It was like looking into a mirror, seeing my heartbroken image staring back at me. She felt my pain, felt it just by looking at me. "Sweetheart…" She wrapped her arms around me in the entryway.

I let my mother hold me. I used her strength as a crutch and accepted the safe place she offered. I hadn't seen her since Bones left because I preferred my bubble of isolation. But I knew she'd been thinking about me, worrying about me constantly. "Hey, Mama."

She ran her hand down my hair, feeling the soft strands along my back. She rested her head against mine, her natural smell surrounding me, reminding me of my childhood.

I didn't want to make today about me. My heartbreak was irrelevant. My family had been patient with me for the last month. My brother would normally be harsher with me, but since he knew I was struggling, he let a lot of my behavior slide.

When I'd taken enough advantage of my mother's comfort, I pulled back. "I want today to be about Conway and Sapphire, not me." I held her gaze with all the confidence I could muster. "So let's not talk about it. We should all be happy today. I'm getting a sister, you're getting a daughter. We have so much to be thankful for." I didn't want to take away my parents' joy today. Their only son was getting married, and it should be an exciting time for them.

"Alright," she whispered. "But your father is having a hard time being happy when he's so worried about you…and your relationship." She rubbed her hand up and down my arm. "I know this is hard for you, but your father loves you more than anything in this world…including me. He always puts you before himself."

"I know…"

"Then make this right with him."

"I'm not ready…"

Her eyes crinkled with sadness. "Then make sure he knows you love him and you forgive him. But you need some time to bounce back. I haven't seen him this low in a long time."

I didn't want my father to be in pain, even if he was wrong about Bones. "I'll go talk to him."

She squeezed my arm. "That's a good idea. I know this is hard for you…just remember it's hard for him too."

I made my way upstairs and stopped on the second floor where my brother's childhood bedroom was. I tapped on the door with my knuckles and heard him welcome me inside. He obviously hadn't been expecting me because he looked surprised to see me. He was already in a suit even though it was still a few hours before the ceremony started. I'd seen him in a suit hundreds of times, but he'd never looked quite as good as he did then. "You look handsome, Con."

He rose from the chair and adjusted his tie down his chest. He only gave a slight nod in acknowledgment of my words. Our get-together ended abruptly last night, and it was hard to interact without thinking about it.

"I'm sorry about last night, Con. I didn't mean to—"

"Forget it. I know you're going through a hard time right now." He let me off the hook so easily, and that wouldn't happen under normal circumstances.

"I'm not sorry for what I said because I know I'm right, but I'm sorry for yelling at you, arguing with you the night before your big day. Truth is, I look up to you, Conway. I think you're a great man, and I'm very proud of you. I love you so much, and not just because I have to. You're the greatest brother I ever could have asked for…" I kept my composure, but my eyes started to water with a hint of tears. "Sapphire made you into an even better man, and I know the little one will too. I'm very happy for you."

His coldness turned into warmth, and the walls he'd erected around his heart suddenly came down. His eyes lightened in happiness, and the rigid way he held his shoulders slipped away. He extended his hand to me, silently beckoning me toward him.

I moved into his chest and rested my face against his muscular frame, letting my brother wrap his thick arms around me. It was nice to be held by my family. There was no greater feeling than this kind of unconditional love.

"Thanks for saying that. I appreciate it."

"And Mama didn't make me."

He chuckled. "I know. And I love you too. It kills me to see you go through this. I wish I could make it better."

"I know…but today isn't about me." I pulled away and looked into his face. "It's about you and Sapphire, and I'm very happy to be celebrating. So let's not talk about me anymore. Let's talk about you." I forced myself to smile, and I noticed the happiness followed immediately. "Nervous?"

He dropped his hands and then adjusted his cuff links, a ghost of a smile on his lips. "Have you seen the woman I'm about to marry? No, I'm definitely not nervous." He grinned in his typically arrogant way.

"Come on," I said. "Be serious."

"I'm fine."

I raised an eyebrow, knowing there was more to the story.

"What do you want me to say?" he asked with a chuckle. "I never thought I would get married, but here I am."

"And you want to get married, right?"

He adjusted his cuff links again. "The idea of being a father and a husband is a little scary, but Father gave me some advice. I feel like I've already grown into those roles, so everything should be fine. I guess that's what scares me about getting married… being good enough for my family."

My brother wore an indifferent façade most of the time, lacking emotion and compassion about almost all things, but I knew there was a sensitive side underneath all the muscle, success, and scotch. "You are, Con."

"I've messed up in the past…as you know. Now that I'm this person, I don't like who I used to be." He moved his hands into his pockets. "I never want to be that man again. And I still want to be better than what I am now…"

"Sapphire loves you exactly as you are, Con."

"I know," he said. "But I still want to be better. I'll always want to be better for her."

Our tender moment was ruined when the door opened and Carter walked inside. "We still have time to hit a strip club and send you off in style." He wore dark jeans and a collared blue shirt, his dark hair and eyes standing out. He wore a nice watch on his wrist along with dress shoes. He walked up to Conway and patted him on the shoulder. "You look good. But not as good as the bride, I hear." He winked.

The corner of Conway's mouth rose in a smile. "I don't take offense to that."

I let the men talk in private by leaving the room and heading to the third floor. Since my father hadn't appeared around the house, I knew there was only one place he could be—in his study drinking scotch.

I approached his study door and knocked. "Can I come in?"

Father paused before answering, recognizing my voice through the solid wood instantly. "Yes."

I walked inside and saw him sitting at his desk, a bottle and a glass in front of him. The fireplace was empty because it was too warm for a fire at this time of year. Throughout the winter season, my father always had a fire burning in the hearth. This was supposed to be a place where he could work in peace, but I'd never seen him do anything for the winery in here. Instead, it seemed to be just a place where he could drink in peace.

He didn't look at me, his eyes on the fireplace even though there weren't any flames to watch. "Conway is in his room. Your mother is in the kitchen." He grabbed his glass and took a drink.

I hated seeing my father this way, morose and empty. He acted the same way when he was angry, but he didn't have that blank expression in his eyes, not like he did now.

I walked to the front of his desk and sat in one of the leather armchairs that faced him.

His eyes finally flicked to my face.

"Are you going to offer me a drink?"

He straightened in his chair, a quiet sigh coming from his lips. "It's a little early."

I cocked an eyebrow. "And it's not a little early for you?"

The corner of his mouth rose in a smile, the same way Conway's had. "I started drinking a few hours ago."

"I've been awake since three, so I'm ready for it."

He didn't make another protest and poured the liquor into a glass. He pushed it to the edge of the desk. "It's strong."

I took a long drink, not grimacing at all as it slid down my throat and hit my stomach. "I'm used to it." That was all Bones ever drank. I hardly saw him without a glass in his hand. He drank in his office, at dinner, and when we lay on the couch together in the evenings.

My father probably knew why I was used to it, but he didn't make a comment about it. "Was there something you needed?"

I stared at the ghostly demeanor of my father. Depressed and scared, he wasn't himself when our relationship was so damaged. He'd never been an emotional person, had never shed a tear in front of me. He was hard like steel, unaffected by everything. The only time he seemed to soften was when it came to my mother, but even then, it wasn't obvious. "I don't hate you, Father. I love you more than words can say, and I would take a bullet for you in a heartbeat." I held his gaze as I spoke, meaning every word from the bottom of my heart.

He controlled his reaction as best he could, but his eyes softened against his will. The relief entered his gaze, and his shoulders weren't as tense as they were a second ago. His fingers relaxed around his glass, and his breathing became softer. "That means a lot to me... except that last part. I would rather die a million times than let anything bad happen to you. I will always make sacrifices for you. Don't you ever make a sacrifice for me." He picked up his glass and took a drink. "Your mother told me you would come around...I'm glad you did. It's all I've been thinking about."

I felt guilty for hurting him, but I still couldn't change the way I felt about the situation. "There's nothing you could ever do to make me hate you. Nothing you could do to make me stop loving you. You'll always be my father, and because of that, I'll always love and respect you. My family means everything to me. That's why I'm still here. But...I still don't agree with what you did. I don't think you're being fair. And I think you're being hypocritical and sexist."

The softness that was in his eyes just a moment ago disappeared. His gaze hardened, staring me down like an enemy. "So, we aren't okay, then?"

"I'm still hurt. I just wanted you to know that I'm still your daughter, and I love you very much."

He released the glass and leaned back in his chair. A sigh escaped his throat, and he looked out the window, avoiding my gaze. His happiness disappeared like a drop of water on a hot day. He turned back to me. "I don't know what you want me to say, *tesoro*. I stand by my decision and won't change my mind. We're at a stalemate."

My father claimed he wanted to protect me, that I would be happier because of this decision, but all I'd felt was utter heartbreak. "What exactly are you protecting me from, Father? Not being with Griffin has hurt me far more than anything he did while we were together."

He tilted his head slightly, his eyes narrowing in anger. "It will pass."

"Maybe. But I'm never going to love another man the way I loved him. My future husband will always be second-best."

"You'll change your mind when you meet him. You've only been in love once—"

"How many times have you been in love?"

Like a lit piece of wood, the fire in his eyes was slowly starting to rise into an inferno. "Once."

"Mama was the one, and you knew she was the one. End of story. Griffin is the one to me."

He shook his head slightly. "I'm not going to change my mind, Vanessa. You should drop this."

I'd never been so frustrated with my father. He'd punished me when I was a child, and that never upset me the way this did. We'd disagreed in the past, but it was never this intense. "Sapphire told me everything about her and Conway." I'd never planned on throwing that in his face, but I didn't have any other option. Today was my brother's wedding day, and it was the worst time to have this argument, but I couldn't keep it in any longer.

My father gave nothing away, his expression exactly the same as before.

"She told me he bought her, demanded sex from her, and kept her as a prisoner."

My father's breathing increased slightly, but he kept up his guarded expression. He knew this was the smoking gun, all the evidence I needed to prove his decision was wrong.

"How is he any different from Griffin?" I snapped.

Silence.

"How?" I pressed. "Sapphire didn't have a family,

and he took advantage of that. He practically turned her into a slave. He took her virginity because he paid for it. So you're going to sit there and tell me that's perfectly okay? That Sapphire should still marry him? What's the difference?"

He clenched his jaw, his eyes darkening.

"What's the damn difference, Father?" I couldn't keep my voice down, my rage escalating. "It's okay because Conway is the one committing the crime? He's guilty of exactly the same thing, but you look the other way. Sapphire is an innocent, kind woman, and she's marrying the man who locked her up in his house for six months. You're okay with that?"

"Vanessa—"

"You're a fucking hypocrite."

My father's expression hardened because I'd never cursed at him like that before. Speechless, he couldn't think of anything to say.

"It's okay because Conway changed. He fell in love with Sapphire and became the man she deserved. That's exactly what Griffin did. He's a new man now—because of me. You can't approve of this wedding and tell Griffin he can't be with me. It's wrong—and you know it."

When his fingers pulled together and made a fist, I knew he was pissed. He rested his hand against his jawline, his furious eyes glued to my face. He was sheathing his anger, controlling himself before exploding. After what seemed like minutes, he lowered his hand and spoke. "Yes. It is hypocritical."

He agreed with me, but judging by his harsh tone, he wasn't going to change his mind. My reasoning seemed to anger him even more.

"It's hypocritical, but I don't give a damn if it is. You are my daughter. That's the difference between you and Sapphire. I'm your father, and I'm a very powerful man who doesn't hesitate to take down my enemies. I've slit the throat of dozens of men and shot them point-blank." He pressed his finger to the top of the desk. "I've worked my ass off to give you this life that you take for granted. I don't accept anything less than the best—and neither will you. I may not be a king, but any man who wants you will treat you like a princess. Sapphire doesn't have a family, but if she did, they wouldn't like Conway either. But that's the difference between you two—you do have a family. You have a father who will fight for you until the day he dies. I will not give up until you have the whole fucking world, Vanessa. My daughter gets the best. That's the end of the fucking story. Be angry. Hate me. I don't care." His eyes darkened even more. "I love you and Conway more than anything else in the world, and I will do the right thing for both of you until I take my last breath. Griffin's father killed my sister. Do you understand how difficult that was for me to look past?"

I didn't say anything, knowing it would be stupid to speak.

"His father raped my wife." His voice rose in intensity, spit flying from his mouth. "Do you have any idea how hard that was for me to let go? But I did—for you. He told me he's fucked prostitutes, he's killed people for money, and he wanted to kill my entire family—and I still let that go. I looked past all of that for you." His chest rose and fell at an exponential rate. It seemed like he might flip over the desk at any moment and smash it to pieces. I'd seen my father angry, but never quite like this. "But I will not look past this. Do you understand me?" He rose to his feet and slammed both of his palms against the desk. "I. Never. Will."

I wore a brave face for as long as I could, but the moisture was starting to flood my eyes. I was heartbroken for so many reasons. Hearing my father yell at me like that made my stomach tighten in knots. He used to be the man I turned to for everything, and now we were screaming at each other like enemies on a battlefield. I told him he was being hypocritical, but that didn't mean a damn thing to him. But what caused me the most pain was the undeniable truth right in front of me—that Griffin and I were really over.

My father would never change his mind.

It was done.

We were done.

I RETREATED to my childhood bedroom so I could let my tears fall in private. I didn't want Sapphire to worry about me. I didn't want Carmen to comfort me. I didn't want my brother to think about me again since today was his special day. Normally, I would turn to my mother, but she was busy preparing for the ceremony.

And I didn't want her to feel sad either.

Everyone should be happy today.

I sat on the foot of the bed and felt the tears fall into my hands. My makeup smeared, but thankfully, I had extra so I could clean up. I remembered sleeping in this bed while talking to Bones on the phone. At the time, I didn't know how I felt about him. But I knew I missed him, knew I wanted to talk to him.

I wished I could pick up the phone and call him right now.

But that would just make it harder for him, for both of us.

I did my best to control my breathing and silence my tears. There would be plenty of time for my sadness later, when I was alone in my apartment in Florence. Right now, I should be celebrating this wonderful moment in my life, my future niece or nephew and my new sister. I didn't want to be selfish, make this day about me. So I took a deep breath, closed my eyes, and tried to clear my thoughts. My throat still burned with the urge to cry, and I tasted the strong bite of salt on my tongue.

Stop, Vanessa.

Crying wouldn't change anything.

I did my best to convince my father to let Bones and me be together. There was nothing more I could do.

It was time to let it go.

Knock. Knock. Knock. My father cracked the door without waiting for me to invite him inside. He looked at me through the opening, grief and anger mixed in his eyes.

I quickly wiped my cheeks with my fingertips. "I'm coming. I was just going to do my makeup—"

He stepped inside and shut the door behind him. Then he took a seat beside me on the bed, his weight making the mattress shift. He rested his arms on his thighs, his torso shifting forward. He stared at his hands, his fingers stitching together. Silence passed, but it wasn't palpable with anger.

I forced myself to stop crying, feeling uncomfortable doing it in front of someone besides Bones.

My father massaged his knuckles on his left hand. "*Tesoro*…I don't want it to be this way. I hate yelling at you. I hate this distance that's grown between us. We used to be so close. Now our relationship is different… and I hate that."

"I hate it too."

He sighed quietly. "I was scared to have Conway. But when you came along, I was even more scared. Having a daughter is so much different from having a son. I want to protect you more, coddle you more. Just because Conway is a man doesn't mean I should assume that he can take care of himself and you can't. You're a very strong and smart woman…I couldn't be prouder of you. But because of that reason, I want to take care of you. I never want you to change. I never want a man to hurt you and shatter you."

I moved my hand to his forearm.

He glanced at my hand before he rested his hand on top. "This is what I want…us."

"We'll always be us, Father. Nothing will ever change that."

He closed his eyes for a brief moment, like that

meant the world to him. "Thank you, *tesoro*. Being a parent is the hardest job in the world. One day, you'll understand that when you have your own children. You'll want to do the right thing for them…always."

"I know you're always trying to do the right thing."

He squeezed my hand. "Are we okay, then?"

My father had made up his mind, and he wouldn't change it. I would be forced to move on from Bones and start over. He was the love of my life, and he would always be the love of my life. But if my family refused to accept him, the relationship would only bring me pain. I wanted a husband whom my father loved like a son. I wanted him to be part of our family, to be friends with Conway. I wanted the Barsetti family to grow, not get smaller. "We're always okay, Father."

He turned his head toward me and kissed me on the forehead. "I love you, *tesoro*." He turned forward again and pulled his hand away.

I rested my head on his shoulder. "I love you too."

"Your mother is the first woman I've ever loved. She's the love of my life, everything to me. I've always been a man who needs the sky, the soil, and the sun to be happy, maybe a glass of scotch here and there. But your mother became all of that…she became everything that makes me happy. I didn't think my heart could grow anymore, that I was capable of loving anything besides her. It took so long just for me to find her. But then you came along…and I loved you instantly. You became the sky, the soil, and the sun. You became my everything." He lifted both of his hands and cupped his fingers. "From the second I held you…I knew there was another woman I loved more than your mother."

My eyes started to water, but for a different reason.

"I want you to be with a man who loves you more than I do. And you'll find him, *tesoro*."

SIX

Conway

It was a beautiful spring day. The roses in the garden were bright and lively, and the olive trees were in full bloom. The grass had been neatly trimmed the day before, and the shady spot beneath the oak trees was the perfect place to marry my muse.

It was just me standing in front of the gazebo, in a black suit with a matching tie. Mama pinned a flower to my jacket, a soft pink that complemented the beautiful day. Muse was so pregnant that she couldn't wear heels anymore, so Lars hemmed her dress a little shorter so she could walk barefoot across the grass covered in pink rose petals. She'd wanted to get married sooner, before her stomach became too big, but I thought the timing worked out perfectly.

She'd never looked as beautiful as she did now.

There wasn't even a slight hint of a breeze, and the world was completely quiet. It was one of the things I loved about growing up in this house. It was away from the city and the road, so all you could hear was nature and the sounds of the grape leaves shifting in the wind.

There was nowhere else I'd rather get married.

Mama was dressed in a blue dress with the same flower pinned to the front. She walked up to me, her eyes wet like they were earlier that day. She'd never been an emotional person, hardly ever shedding a tear as the years passed. Strong like my father, she chose to be fearless. But today, those rules didn't seem to apply.

She stopped in front of me and gripped my biceps, her chin tilted up as she looked at me. I was over a foot taller than her, twice her size, and she seemed so small in comparison. "My son…" She moved into me and rested her face against my chest. "So happy for you…"

I wrapped my arms around my mom and held her.

Uncle Cane and Aunt Adelina sat in the row of chairs with Lars and Carter and Carmen. We had a small family, but it was nice having it just be us. My father stood on the other side of me, watching us together.

"I know, Mama." I rubbed her back. "Thanks for raising me to be a man."

She chuckled slightly and swiped a finger under her

eye. "A good man." She took a deep breath to steady her tears. "And a man I love so much."

"I love you too."

She pulled away and composed herself as much as possible. "It feels like it was just yesterday when your father and I got married in this very spot. And it seems like yesterday when I sat on the porch and told him I was pregnant with you. Now here you are…starting your own family. I feel very…lucky." She rose on her tiptoes and kissed me on the cheek before she sat down with Vanessa.

Father turned to me next. He rested his hand on my back, a smile in his eyes. "I don't think there's any advice I have left to give you."

"I don't know about that. I'm not a father yet… I'm sure I'll need some help."

"You never needed my help becoming the successful man you are now. I'm sure you'll be fine. But I'm here if you ever need anything." He patted my back before he pulled away. "I never had anyone to ask for advice when I had you. I had to figure it out on my own."

"I think you did okay."

He chuckled. "I did more than okay. I have two perfect children. I wouldn't change anything about either one of you."

"Not even Vanessa's brattiness?"

He laughed, knowing I was joking. "Not even that."

"At least I have a good role model to look up to."

He patted my back before he stepped away. "Thanks, son. Something I learned about raising both of you…something I learned just today…as long as you love your kids, everything will be alright."

"That doesn't sound too difficult."

He shook his head. "It's not." He walked away and took the seat beside my mother, his arm moving around her shoulders as they waited for me to marry the love of my life. He gave me a slight nod of approval, along with a smile.

The harpist began to play, and the music started. I turned my attention to the house, where a beautiful woman in a white dress emerged. Glowing like the setting sun, she stepped onto the grass in her elegant white dress, her baby bump as lovely as the rest of her. She held a bundle of pink roses, and her eyes were stuck on me like I was the only person there. She looked at me the way I looked at her, like there was no one else in the world that really mattered.

She came closer to me, her movements just as elegant as they were on the catwalk. Her smile was true and radiant, but her eyes welled with emotional tears. Her hair was in large curls that trailed down her front, and the diamond necklace around her throat looked familiar, but I couldn't recall where I'd seen it before.

As she came closer, the world seemed to stop. I'd never imagined what my wedding day would be like. I thought marriage was for people who couldn't make it on their own. They needed someone to depend on, someone to give them self-worth. But once I'd fallen in love with Muse, I couldn't imagine my life without her. She made me weak, but in a good way.

My life was about to be different forever. I would have to love and protect two people instead of one, and I wasn't included in that number. Muse made me feel insignificant, because her life was much more important than mine. I used to be arrogant and selfish, thinking I had the world in the palm of my hand. And then this woman auditioned to be a model, and nothing was ever the same.

I realized I would do anything for her, even sacrifice my own life.

My body wasn't hit with doubts. I was strong and confident like always, eager to make this woman my wife.

To call her Mrs. Barsetti.

I wanted to smother her with my life, wealth, and protection. I wanted to put her on a pedestal and make all her dreams come true. I wanted to give her as many children as she wanted, especially when I got to enjoy her looking that way for nine months.

She approached me, her eyes coated with unshed tears. She seemed to be deep in thought the way I was, thinking about our lives together and the family we would make. When she reached me, she stepped closer to me, her face moving to my chest.

My arms wrapped around her, and I held her in front of the priest and my family. I should take her hand and face her so I could say the vows that would bind us together forever. But now, I needed to hold her, to take this moment to cherish the woman I'd already committed to for the rest of my life. "You sure you want to marry me?"

She looked up from my chest, her tears thickening into drops. "Never been so sure of anything in my life."

FIVE HOURS LATER, we arrived in Positano, a small village on the Amalfi coast. Just an hour away from Naples, it was a scenic route along the mountainside. With windy turns with gorgeous views of the Mediter-ranean, it was a beautiful sight—even in the darkness.

I would have preferred to fly, but Muse was far too pregnant for that. At seven months, she couldn't board a plane. So I drove through the night, letting her sleep in the passenger seat, still in her wedding dress. I advised her to take it off for the drive.

But she wanted me to take it off.

We checked in to our hotel, a luxurious place in the heart of the city. Our honeymoon suite had an eye-catching view of the harbor with the sailboats. I carried her over the threshold and into the large suite that we would probably never leave.

I lay her on the bed, her white gown still as stunning as it was earlier.

She was tired on the drive, but now that we were alone in our suite, she was wide awake. She looked up at me with her hair across the bed, her eyes bright and playful. I was leaning over her, so she ran her palms up my chest to my tie. She slowly loosened it, her eyes locked on mine.

I watched her as her fingers worked the silk, my cock already hard in my slacks because I knew what was coming next. I'd been waiting all day for this moment. I didn't realize it at the time, but I'd been waiting my whole life for this moment.

She pulled the silk from around my neck then unbuttoned my collared shirt, slowly making her way to my stomach. As each button came unfastened, our breathing grew deeper and louder. My eyes never left hers, and I felt the intensity stretch between us, the desire and the desperation.

I couldn't wait to be inside her.

Inside my wife.

Fuck, I have a wife.

When my shirt was undone, she pushed my jacket off my shoulders with the shirt. Everything hit the tile floor with a dull thud.

Her hands explored my chest, pausing over my beating heart. I'd worked out hard that week, taking on more weight than I ever had. I wanted my ripped body to be in perfect shape for tonight, so she could enjoy me the way I enjoyed her.

She moved to my slacks next, unbuckling my belt and then opening the zipper. She pushed them down, making my thick cock emerge. With a slight tint of red, he was hard and stretched, ready to be inside the cunt that officially belonged to me.

I would just fuck her like that, but not tonight. Now I wanted to peel off that dress, remove every piece of clothing, and make her come the second I was inside her. I loved her pregnancy because it made her even hornier than she used to be.

She couldn't get enough of me.

I pulled her to her feet and then undid the thousands of buttons along the back. I unbuttoned each one, moving until I reached the top of her ass. I pushed the dress over her shoulders and watched it crumple to the floor.

Beautiful.

In a little white thong, she looked as untouched as ever. I was the only man she'd ever had. And I would be the only man she'd ever have.

I pressed kisses from the back of her neck down to her shoulder. My hands moved to her thong, and I twisted it in my fingertips, playing with the material. I forced myself to slow down even though I was anxious to be inside her. I couldn't skip to the end when the beginning was more important. I didn't want to fuck her, but I wanted to be inside her as quickly as possible.

I kept kissing her, listened to her breathe. And then I worked her panties, pulling them down until her perfect ass appeared. Her round belly was her sexiest feature, full of the life I'd put inside her. Her birth control couldn't stop me from knocking her up, from putting a baby inside her.

I was prouder of that than any of my other accomplishments.

I knelt as I pulled down her panties, moving them to her ankles and kissing her as I went. This woman had brought me to my knees more times than I could count—and I never minded one bit.

How could I?

I turned her around and pressed my face close to hers, but I didn't kiss her, regardless of how much my lips ached for that beautiful mouth. I paused, letting the intensity increase between us. The intimacy was hot, the way we looked at each other in expectation. I'd already taken her virginity once, but I felt like I was about to do it again.

My cock twitched.

"Mrs. Barsetti." I guided her back to the bed, my bare feet planted on the tile floor. I placed her at the very edge of the mattress, her sexy ass hanging over. Her stomach was so big that it was difficult to make love in any other position.

But I didn't mind.

I pinned her knees near her stomach and then pressed my cock inside. She was soaking wet, tight, and absolutely perfect. A quiet moan of pleasure escaped my lips, and my cock twitched once I was inside.

I moved all the way, hitting her until only my balls hung out.

She dug her nails into my arms and took a deep breath. "Con…" She bit her bottom lip and took a deep breath, her nipples hard like diamonds.

"Mrs. Barsetti." I slowly started to move, my eyes on hers. My hands gripped her hips, and I dragged her toward me slightly, hitting her deep with every thrust. I took her gently, taking pleasure in the sight of her tits and her stomach. My hands moved to her belly next, where the baby we made together was growing deep inside. Knowing I put this life inside her aroused me in a carnal way I couldn't explain.

Her hands rested on top of mine as she took my length over and over again. She continued to bite her lip and moan for me, her breaths coming out deep and shaky. There wasn't just desire in her eyes, but overwhelming love that could block out the sun. This woman loved me despite my imperfections. She loved me because of the man I was, not the size of my wallet or package.

I already wanted to come inside her wet cunt. Her pregnancy made my threshold even lower. Every time I was with her, it was the best sex I'd ever had. Now that she was my wife, I could barely control myself at all.

She closed her eyes for a brief moment, her mouth opening. "God…"

I shoved myself deeper inside her, plunging into the tight pussy that belonged exclusively to me. I'd been the only one to take her this way, to both fuck her and make love to her. My pure bride was my exclusive property, only touched by me.

She tightened around me, just the way my fingers

tightened around my dick when I came. Musical moans erupted from her lips, high-pitched and beautiful. With closed eyes and a gaping mouth, she looked like a woman well pleased. She gripped my wrists and rocked with my movements, taking my dick deep and hard. "Con…"

I rubbed my thumb against her clit, making her writhe even more. I pushed her over the edge, made her orgasm last a lifetime. I watched her tits shake, watched her pant from the ecstasy. Focusing on her pleasure controlled mine. Like a good husband, I managed to wait until she was completely done before I allowed myself to finish. After a few pumps, my head exploded inside her, and I pumped her with my come, dumping a pile of it deep inside her. We'd agreed not to sleep together before the wedding, and now my body was catching up. I gripped her swollen tits with my palms as I finished, feeling my cock thicken as I released. When every drop was exactly where it should be, I started to soften. But the pleasure seemed to continue on after my dick lost its hardness, because the euphoria seemed to exist beyond the physical satisfaction of sex. It seemed to continue on indefinitely because of the connection between us, because of the bond between our souls. Intertwined and locked together, we were a single person. We made a life together, something that would carry on after we were dead and gone. My pleasure wouldn't stop because I was happy, happier than I'd ever been my entire life. Finding Muse completed me, filled in the holes I never realized I had. She was my whole world, my reason for living. My purpose used to lie in my work, the success of my business and my designs. I used to work day and night, obsessing over my next piece and the world's reaction to it. But once Muse was mine, she became my priority. Work didn't seem important anymore, more like an afterthought.

Now my wife was my whole world.

And the baby we made together.

My family was everything to me.

They say at some point you turn into your parents. I always thought my father and I were distinctly different, despite our physical similarities. But now I realized I'd become just like him, walking away from a life I used to think was important because I'd found something so much more vital.

I found my family.

SEVEN

Bones

───────────

When I opened my eyes, I saw the broken glass
everywhere.

My head was against the doorframe, and when I
squinted my eyes, I could see the flickering lights from
the police and the medics. Conversation erupted
around me, men speaking over the radio. My safety belt
cut into my chest and shoulder, but my weight was too
heavy to keep me in place. The steering wheel was in
front of me. Blood dripped down my face. My body
was sore, like I'd just collided with a massive tree trunk.

I couldn't remember what happened.

The men removed the passenger door from its
hinges so they could get to me inside. My truck had
been turned completely on its side, leaving me buried
inside. I heard a man's voice speak to me.

"Sir? Are you awake? Talk to me."

"Hmm?" I could barely get the sound out of my mouth. I was too drunk to function. I'd never been this drunk in my life. I was so drunk I couldn't even remember drinking.

"He's awake," the man said to the others. "We're going to get you out. Stay still."

Like I could move anyway.

I closed my eyes and felt myself slip away. The darkness descended, and then I was gone.

———

THE NEXT TIME I opened my eyes, I was in a hospital bed. The gentle beep of the monitor acted as a strange form of music. I was on my back, an IV in my arm, and my large body was fitted with a gown. I noticed the small TV on the wall, took in the white colors of the hospital room, and then spotted the man sitting at my bedside.

Max.

I opened my eyes farther, squinting against the harsh fluorescent lights, and focused on him. "Max?"

He didn't look relieved to see me. In fact, he looked pissed. "Yeah. It's me."

I dragged my hand down my face and looked around, unsure what I was even looking for. I vaguely remembered the accident, remembered the men who yanked me out of the truck. The memory of the pole came back to me, when I hit it head on. "What's going on?"

"You were an asshole," he snapped. "That's what's going on."

I turned back to Max, seeing the rage on his face that I heard in his voice.

"I knew you weren't okay…"

I looked at the monitor with my vitals, but I didn't understand any of the numbers, so I looked away. It took me a while to come back to myself, to remember where I was and how I got there.

"What the fuck were you thinking?" He stood up, his shoulders hunched with rage. "They had to pump your stomach because you had so much alcohol in your system they thought you might die. What the fuck, Bones?"

I remembered the bar. I remembered the second bar…and the third. I remembered being cut off by one bartender before I headed to another. Most of it was a blur, but I definitely remember losing my mind…and my control.

"You smashed into a pole. No one else was hurt."

That was good news.

"You broke a few ribs, got a concussion, and you have a nasty cut in your forehead. But the doctors say you're going to be fine…thankfully."

Why didn't that make me feel better? Why did I wish I was dead instead?

Max's rage slowly drifted away as he stared at me. He must have seen the defeat in my gaze and knew yelling at me wouldn't make any kind of difference. I'd already hit rock bottom. He couldn't make me feel worse. "I didn't know it was this bad, man."

I looked away, unable to meet his gaze. The past five weeks had been spent in isolation. The only company I had was my booze. It seemed to blur my thoughts, so I kept drinking because it helped me think about nothing at all.

Helped me not think about her.

"Talk to me." He came closer to the bed, standing over me. Now he looked like a concerned friend…a concerned brother.

"I'm fine." My voice came out surprisingly strong for how weak I was. "I'm fine…"

"Cut the shit." His eyes narrowed. "You aren't fine. I'm not letting you out of here until you say otherwise.

You have a serious problem, Bones. If you don't get it fixed, I'm not letting you out of my sight."

I turned my head the other way, not wanting to see his disappointment. "I got carried away...didn't realize how much I drank."

"Bullshit. You knew exactly how much you drank."

"Maybe at the beginning of the night...but not the end."

"Were you trying to get yourself killed?" he demanded.

It didn't sound like the worst thing in the world.

When I didn't answer, he spoke again. "No more booze for you. I'm serious."

I wanted to argue, but after all the damage I'd done, I knew he was right.

"You have a problem—a big one."

I had no self-control. I had no purpose. I didn't realize how much Vanessa meant to me until she was gone. I knew I loved her, would die for her, but I hadn't realized just how much she did for me...how she made me better. Now that she was gone...I had nothing to live for. "I know..."

"Until you get better, no more. Not a drop."

I didn't care if I lived or died, but I did care about Max and the guys. If something happened to me, they would never get over it. We were a family. It was the first time in my life I was embarrassed by something I'd done. It was the first time I felt like apologizing for a crime I'd committed.

"Understand me?"

I nodded. "Am I going to jail tonight?"

"No. No one is pressing charges."

Looked like our arrangement with the police was still intact.

"If you hurt someone…it might have been a different story. Thankfully, you didn't."

"How's my truck?"

"In worse shape than you are."

I nodded even though I didn't know why.

Max sighed before he pulled up a chair and sat down. "I didn't call her…but do you want me to?"

There was nothing I wanted more than to see her walk through that door with tears in her eyes. Her love was the only thing that could make me better. Any other time I was down, I got lost in pussy. But I hadn't done that because I wasn't ready to be with another woman, to really say goodbye to the woman I loved. "No."

"You're sure?"

I nodded. "It'll just make it harder…for both of us." I hadn't called her even though I almost did a few times.

I hadn't gone to Florence to check on her because I knew she didn't need my protection anymore. I hadn't given into my urges to be with her because nothing had changed. And if I saw that beautiful face, I would have to start all over…and these past five weeks had been hard enough. I didn't want to think about how hard it'd been for her. It would just make me feel like shit.

Max didn't press it. "Stay with me for a while."

"I want to be alone." I'd always been alone. I preferred solitude. But now that Vanessa was gone, the isolation was hollow. I missed the sound of her footsteps down the hallway. I missed seeing drops of paint on her clothes. I missed her smell on my sheets. I missed the way she clung to me in the middle of the night even when it wasn't cold.

Max didn't press that either. "I've got to make sure you stop drinking."

"I will, Max," I said coldly. "You don't need to check on me."

"You bet your ass I'm going to check on you. If you let it get this bad, it doesn't give me much confidence that you can change it so easily."

"I can. I'm not proud of what happened."

"You shouldn't be. The guys were worried…they were here a few hours ago."

I knew Max had been there the entire time without even asking. "I'm sorry."

Max's eyes widened slightly, surprised by what I said.

Apologies didn't come easily from me, if they ever came at all. Even if I were wrong, I would never admit it. But what I'd done was horrific. "I'm sorry for being so stupid. I'm sorry for being so weak. It won't happen again." I didn't look at him when I spoke, unable to meet his gaze. Shame washed over me like a river. It stung at the time, but it also cleansed me.

Max gripped my shoulder and gave me a gentle squeeze. "I'm glad you're alright, Bones. Wouldn't know what to do without you…"

Max and the guys were all the family I had left, and I felt like an asshole for taking it for granted. If Vanessa knew what I did, she would shoot me again. But her disappointment would be far worse than a gunshot wound. "So, how long do I have to stay here?"

"A few days."

I sighed under my breath.

He chuckled. "Don't expect me to feel bad for you. You put yourself in here."

"True."

"But I'll keep you company, man."

"You don't have to do that, Max. I know you're busy."

"I am busy," he said with attitude. "But if we switched places, I know you would never leave my side. And even if that wasn't true, I'm still not going anywhere. You're my brother...and this is where I belong."

EIGHT

Vanessa

Six weeks had come and gone, and it was the first time I started to feel a little better.

As in, I didn't feel the urge to cry anymore.

The last conversation I had with my father gave me closure. It gave me acceptance. I knew Bones and I would never be together again, and that finality shut the door on the relationship for good. I did everything I possibly could to keep him, and now that I knew our love would never work, I could move on without wondering if there was something else I could have done.

That didn't mean I was over him. It didn't mean I stopped loving him. It just made me realize I had to move forward...without him. My close relationship with my father reminded me what was important in life. When Bones first told me he loved me, I rejected him because I knew it would never work.

That instinct had been right.

I should have listened to my gut.

My father claimed I would love someone else someday, that he would be everything I wanted. I had a hard time believing that, believing there was a man out there I'd want for the rest of my life. The only reason I might ever want anyone was because of the way he connected with my family. But other than that, I didn't see much hope for a real and passionate relationship.

Bones would always be the one.

I kept busy at my gallery and painted in the apartment upstairs. My paintings were still moody and dark, but as time passed, they lightened in color and became more romantic. They weren't as good as my original work, but I was making progress.

My artwork was therapeutic. It gave me something to focus my thoughts on, and it gave me a way to express myself. I stopped painting Bones as the weeks passed. He popped up in my paintings sometimes, but his appearance became rarer.

I focused on landscapes, particularly Florence. As I explored the city, I found more places I liked. I would take a picture on my phone of a bakery or a cobbled street with a bicycle leaning up against the wall then I would return to my apartment to paint it with my own style.

Those were the paintings that sold the most.

Throughout the day, I would get a handful of customers, but only a few of them would actually buy anything. As time passed, I seemed to get more interest, especially when the summer hit. Tourists came in looking for original artwork to take home and mount on their wall.

It was nice staying busy. Keeping myself occupied helped the throbbing pain in my heart. Carmen suggested I hook up with someone since it'd been almost two months since Bones left. Finding a new guy might help me forget about the old one.

But I still wasn't ready, not even for meaningless sex.

I wondered if Bones had already been with someone else. Judging by his past promiscuity, he'd probably started screwing other people within two weeks of our breakup. Of course, the thought made me jealous and sad, but at the same time, I knew those women didn't mean anything to him. They were just something to cure the loneliness, something to get off to. I was the only woman who would ever mean anything to him—forever.

I hung up a new painting in the gallery, an image

of the city from the outside fields. It showed the beautiful church, the tall buildings, and a few pedestrians on the sidewalk. I took the picture early in the morning, right as the sun rose, and there were only a few cars parked against the curb. It was one of my favorites, a perfect view of the city.

The door to the gallery opened, and heavy footfalls sounded behind me.

I'd stopped hoping that Bones would stop by to check on me. Six weeks had come and gone, and I never heard from him. If he lasted this long without contacting me, then he would never contact me again.

I turned around to see a tall man standing in front of one of my paintings. He wasn't my usual clientele because he was much younger than the people that came in here. He looked to be my brother's age, possibly a few years younger or older. He stood with his hands in the pockets of his dark jeans. The pants hugged his muscled thighs and his tight ass, and his olive green t-shirt stretched across his shoulder blades and over his muscular arms. He had dark skin like mine and black hair that reminded me of my father's. Short and styled, it was simple. I couldn't see his face because he was turned the other way.

For a second, I didn't address him, unsure what I should say. It was rare to see a young man searching for artwork, especially when he was alone. Sometimes young couples came in looking for something to take home since they were on their honeymoon. But everyone else was much older. "Let me know if you need anything." He seemed focused on looking at my paintings, so I didn't want to intrude on his inspection. It was an image of my favorite bakery, a little place that had planters lined with colorful flowers everywhere. They had amazing coffee, but the unique architecture and lively garden made it a painter's dream.

He turned my way slightly, showing his face for the first time. With a hard jawline, masculine cheekbones, and brilliant brown eyes, he was a beautiful Italian man. His expression was hard, like he'd been focused just a moment ago. His eyes settled on me, and slowly, a soft smile formed on his lips. "Thank you. This is the bakery I go to every morning. It's even more stunning in the painting." He turned back to the image, a picture I'd painted just a few days ago.

"It's my favorite place too." I came up to his side slowly, self-conscious that I'd skipped the makeup and threw my hair in a bun. My t-shirt was baggy because of the weight I'd lost, and my jeans started to feel loose too.

His eyes moved across the colors, settling on the planter box full of red geraniums. He appreciated every single inch, studied it like he was looking for something specific. "How much is it?"

I'd just hung it up, so I hadn't had a chance to put up the price. "Nine hundred euro."

He didn't have a reaction to the amount. "I'll take it."

It was the quickest sale I'd ever made. "Really?"

"Absolutely." He lifted the painting off the wall and held it between his large hands. He examined it again, getting another look before he handed it off to me. "It's beautiful. I have just the spot for it."

"That's great. Let me just wrap it up for you."

"No need. I live a few blocks away." He pulled out his wallet and handed me his card.

I took it, paying attention to the name.

Antonio Tassone.

I wasn't sure why I looked or cared, but for some reason, I did. I ran his card and handed it back to him with the receipt. "Thanks for coming in. Enjoy your painting."

"I will." He gave me a handsome smile, the kind that could pick up a woman instantly. His eyes seemed to take me in a moment longer, like he saw something he wanted to remember. Then he carried his painting out of the store and disappeared past the window.

Once he was gone, a pain filled my heart. He was

the first man I found attractive, the first man that I noticed. As if I'd betrayed Bones, the guilt burned in my stomach. I was supposed to move on, but it seemed too soon for that.

I found Antonio attractive. I found him interesting because he liked art—my art.

But I definitely wasn't ready.

I wasn't sure when I would ever be ready.

———

I'D JUST WALKED into my apartment when Carmen knocked on the door behind me.

"Hey, what's up?" I asked when I opened the door.

She was dressed in a red sleeveless dress with sandals. It'd been a hot day in Florence, the summer heat and humidity making everyone sweat, but Carmen didn't seem to be affected by the weather. "Just wanted to take you out for a drink."

I hadn't been out much, choosing to hide within the four walls of my apartment. Carmen had respected my space for a while, knowing I needed to get through this breakup on my own.

But obviously, her patience had run out. "Vanessa, come on," she said as she rolled her eyes. "You need to get out of this apartment."

"I work every day, thank you very much."

She rolled her eyes again, this time harder. "Downstairs. You walk like ten feet."

"Whatever. I'm still working. I actually sold a painting today." To a very handsome man.

"That's great," she said. "Let's go out and celebrate."

My cousin was only trying to cheer me up, so I thought it would be rude to ignore her. "I'm not picking up a guy, so don't force that stunt on me."

"Fine. But if a hot guy asks you out, you have to say yes."

I narrowed my eyes. "No."

"Vanessa—"

"I'm not ready."

"It's been six weeks, woman. Don't you need some action? You must be going crazy going from getting it on with that hot piece of man to now you've got nothing happening. So treat yourself."

I did miss sex. A lot. But I knew it wouldn't be good with anyone else, not when I wasn't in love. "The man who bought that painting today was a great-looking guy."

"Yeah?" she asked with a smile.

"Beautiful man. But I felt so guilty for being attracted to him that I knew it was too soon."

"So you let him walk out and didn't get his number?" she asked incredulously.

I nodded. "I'm not ready."

"It's been six weeks…"

"I know, but that's not long enough for me. I need more time. So whether a hot guy buys me a drink or not, I'm not going home with anyone."

Carmen gave me a sympathetic look along with a nod. "Alright, no pressure. But you should get out anyway. You need to be around other humans, not a bunch of paint and brushes. And you know what? You can help find a hot guy for me."

"Now that, I can do."

I changed, and we left my apartment. We walked up the road a few blocks, both in dresses and heels. We passed the window of an art gallery, and in the very front was a painting that made me stop walking. It was new, because I'd passed this street a few times and never spotted it before.

Carmen kept walking, but she stopped when she realized I wasn't beside her any longer. "What's the holdup?"

I crossed my arms and stared at the painting through the glass. It was an image of Tuscany, of the vineyards in the background and a country home in the foreground. The details of the flowers, the ivy, the olive trees, and the rustic Italian craftsmanship all impressed me. Each flower petal was perfect, the sky was such an idyllic blue, and it perfectly captured the feeling of the countryside in the heat of summer.

It reminded me of my childhood.

It was the kind of painting I'd created dozens of times, but this painting spoke to me on such a deep level.

Carmen stared at it with me, her head slightly tilted. "It's pretty. But I think your paintings are better."

"No such thing as better," I said as I stared at the expert brushstrokes. "This is a masterpiece."

"Are you going to get it?"

"I wonder how much it is…"

Carmen stepped closer to the glass and squinted her eyes. "I can't tell. Can't read the artist's name either. Looks like chicken scratches…"

"They're closed now. But I think I'll come by tomorrow."

"Where are you going to put it?"

"In my living room. Right above the couch."

"Yeah, that will look nice," she said in agreement. "Hope it's not too pricey. You never know how much a painting is gonna cost."

"True. But I think it'll be worth every penny."

I WENT to the gallery down the road around lunchtime and was relieved to see the painting still hanging in the window. It was a large piece, something big enough to draw the focus in my living room. At least it would take the distraction off the painting of Bones…a painting I stared at constantly.

I walked inside, noticing how different the layout was from my gallery. My place had light walls, a hardwood floor, and lots of art lights directly on the pieces. This gallery was much moodier, with black walls, dark floors, and a special type of art light that brought out the intense colors of the paintings. There were no other customers there when I stepped inside.

A woman was working behind the counter. She greeted me with a smile then offered to help me.

"I'm interested in the painting in the window," I said. "It's beautiful."

"Not only beautiful, but special," she said. "It was painted on the first day of summer."

"That was just a week ago."

"Yes. I'm surprised it's still in the window. Paintings go pretty quick here."

Maybe it was just a sales tactic, but I wanted that painting so much, it worked on me. "I grew up in

Tuscany, so the painting really touched me. How much?"

"Twenty-five hundred euros."

That was several times more expensive than my pieces, but the price didn't surprise me. It came with a nice frame, and it was a quality piece of work from a professional. I'd been making decent money selling my work, and since I didn't have rent to pay or even a car payment, money wasn't an issue for me. "I'll take it."

Surprise came over her face, but she quickly hid it away. "That's lovely. Let me ring it up, and I'll wrap it up for you."

"That's not necessary. I live right down the road. I'll just carry it."

"Very well." She guided me to the counter and took my card.

I glanced around the room, looking at the other pieces. They all seemed to possess the same craftsmanship. "Are these all local artists?"

She ran my card through the machine then gave me the receipt to sign. "Local, yes. But it's not a collection of artists. This galley belongs to—" She stopped talking when the door opened. "Actually, here he is now. The artist who painted this lovely piece of work— Antonio Tassone."

My heart fell into my stomach before I even turned

to look at the man I'd met a few days ago. He stopped by my gallery and bought one of my paintings, and here I was, buying one of his. The irony was so overwhelming I didn't know if I should laugh or feel embarrassed. I turned to the door and saw Antonio Tassone walk in, wearing the same casual jeans and t-shirt as the last time I saw him. He filled out his clothing well, having a broad chest that was thick and hard. He was a perfect triangle, his wide shoulders narrowing down to his hips. He was slender and ripped, having a musculature similar to my father and brother. Bones was thick like a beast, and this man was on the leaner side.

When his eyes settled on me, there was a spark of familiarity. He recognized me, and that same lazy smile came over his chiseled jaw. A light amount of scruff sprinkled the area around his lips, like he forgot to shave that morning. With brown eyes the color of hot coffee, he was the kind of man I would normally ask out in a heartbeat.

I kept standing there, unsure what to do or say. I'd never been the kind of person that was intimidated or lost her confidence, but it took me a second to regain my balance, either because I was surprised by the turn of events or because this man was so undeniably fine.

He stopped by the counter, confident as ever. "Excellent choice." He looked at the painting, staring at it fondly like it was one of his children. "I went to the edge of the city first thing in the morning. The morning light in Tuscany is an artist's dream."

I wanted to agree, but I forgot how to talk.

"Here's your card." The woman held it out to me.

That snapped me out of the moment, and I took it. "Thanks."

"Let me wrap this up for you." Antonio moved behind the counter.

"That's not necessary," I said, finally finding my words. "I live two blocks away. I'll carry it." Now I wanted to get out of there as quickly as possible, never to return to this block ever again. Antonio Tassone wasn't only a handsome and charming man, but a very talented artist. The more I liked him, the more I disliked him.

"Really?" he asked. "In that case, I'll carry it for you. It's a bit heavy."

"I can do it," I blurted, sounding rude when I didn't mean to. I quickly spoke again, erasing the damage I caused. "I just mean, I'm stronger than I look…"

"I never doubted your strength, *signorina*." He gripped the painting by both sides of the frame and held it perpendicular to the floor. "So don't doubt my chivalry. You've purchased a very beautiful and expensive piece of work. The least I can do is carry it for you." Antonio looked at me, his eyes starting to smolder with authority. A hint of a smile was on his lips, like he knew he'd gotten his way.

"Okay…" I didn't want to spend any extra time with this man. Not even a second. "I just live two blocks this way." I walked out first and reached the sidewalk.

He emerged behind me, his arm muscles flexing slightly as he held the weight of the painting. There were very few people on the street, so it seemed like just the two of us in this big city.

Together, we walked forward, side by side.

I could barely breathe. My chest ached. So much guilt washed over me. I didn't like being this close to him, being alone with a man like him. It seemed like I was doing something wrong, betraying the man I loved just by being a few inches away from this one.

"Where are you going to put it?" Antonio asked as he walked beside me, over a foot taller than me.

"In my living room."

"I'm flattered." He smiled in a genuine way, the kind that reached his eyes. He looked handsome when he smiled and handsome when he didn't. It didn't matter what his expression was, his beauty never changed.

Instead of letting the silence make things more

awkward, I blurted something out. "I grew up in Tuscany, so your painting really touched me. I walked past your gallery last night, and when I saw your painting, I had to come back and get it."

"Again, I'm flattered." He possessed a deep and masculine voice, and his words flowed like honey. Confident and relaxed, he was comfortable in his own skin.

After two blocks had passed, we stopped at the gallery. "This is me."

He looked at the gallery before his eyebrows rose up his forehead.

"I live in the apartment above the gallery." I didn't walk up the stairs on the side to my apartment, not wanting him to follow me inside my home. This was the farthest I was going to take him.

"Really?" He stared at the gallery for a few more seconds, his brow furrowed like he was trying to piece the puzzle together. "Do you own the gallery?"

"Yeah." I realized he had no idea the painting he bought was mine. He must have thought I was only some woman working behind the counter, just like the woman in his shop. A part of me wanted to lie and pretend the artwork wasn't mine, to deny a connection that we obviously shared. But my lie would catch up with me...sooner or later.

He finally turned back to me, his concentrated expression gone and his handsome smile wide. "That's wonderful. How long have you been here?"

"Only about two months." I took the painting from his hands, wanting to make sure he had no reason to come into my apartment. The last thing I wanted was to be alone with a man behind closed doors. I didn't think anything would happen between us, but it felt too soon—even for that. "Thank you for giving me a hand with this. You're right." I tested the weight. "It's a bit heavy."

He slid his hands into his pockets and didn't offer to carry it up the stairs to my apartment. He must have sensed the boundary I'd placed between us and didn't try to press his chivalry any further.

I wanted to turn away and end this conversation now, before he asked the question I didn't want to answer. "I guess I'll see you around, Mr. Tassone." Keeping it formal was smart. It would keep the distance between us.

"Antonio," he said, the corner of his mouth rising in a smile. "What kind of artists do you carry here? I'd never heard of Vanessa Barsetti before I purchased your painting. Is she a new artist? Her work is remarkable. I don't buy paintings very often, but the moment I saw hers…I felt something."

I forgot to breathe because his compliment meant so much to me. This amazing artist just complimented me…an amateur. I'd dropped out of university to pursue this, but I never really believed in myself. Now this talented man was complimenting me, having no idea I was the one who painted the piece. The second I laid eyes on his painting, I knew I needed to hang it in my home. His work was inspiring, beautiful, and mesmerizing. The fact that someone who created the paintings he did thought my work was any good…was surreal. "She's the only artist that I carry…because she is me. And thank you for your kind words…I'm very touched."

His smile faded away instantly, and the look that replaced it was one I'd never seen before, not on him or anyone else. His coffee-colored eyes stared at me, looking at me in a new way, like he was seeing me for the very first time. His gaze intense and deep, he stared at me like he could see past my face and to everything underneath.

Now, I regretted telling him the truth. The second the words were out of my mouth, everything changed. The connection between us was so obvious that neither one of us could unsee it. Like a bright red line stretched between us. We bought each other's paintings without having any idea the other one created it. We got lost in each other's work, in each other's beauty.

And now we were getting lost in each other.

I didn't want this. I wanted to run away and pretend it never happened. I wished I'd never bought that painting. I wished Carmen and I hadn't walked past the window and spotted it. I wished I'd never allowed Antonio to carry the painting to my apartment.

Now he was staring at me with an intense gaze, his body rigid and strong. His shoulders tightened, and his chest expanded with the deep breath he took. He seemed to let out a quiet sigh, almost in resignation.

I didn't have silent eye contact with anyone like this besides Bones. Those looks were packed with sexual aggression, profound love, and a million other emotions. I didn't want to share that intimacy with anyone else. "I should go... I have somewhere to be. Goodbye, Antonio." I turned away and walked up the stone steps to the apartment above the gallery. I didn't turn back to look at him again, to see the expression on his face as I left. I said goodbye on purpose, to bring a sense of finality to the conversation. I wanted to shut the door on the possibility of seeing him ever again.

But he didn't say goodbye in return.

NINE

Vanessa

After three days passed and I didn't see or hear from Antonio, the fear passed. I had been afraid he would stop by and ask me out, but he never did, to my fortune. Maybe the cold way I turned away and walked into my apartment was a clear sign I wasn't interested.

I hoped I wouldn't see him, at least for a few months.

It'd only been two months since Bones and I broke up. It felt too soon to be with someone else.

It was too soon.

Bones had probably been with other women already, but that didn't matter. It wasn't a competition, and I knew they didn't mean anything to him anyway.

Antonio already meant something to me. When he

painted such a beautiful piece of art that was in my home, it was impossible for him not to have significance to me.

Once the danger passed, I returned to working in my gallery in peace. My life was pretty boring, just work, painting, and staying inside my apartment. I cooked all my meals and never went out, preferring the sanctuary of my apartment. I started to gain some weight back because I was eating normally again, but I still wasn't back to my normal form.

I was downstairs in the gallery taking a picture of a new painting when the door opened and someone came inside. I set down my phone and turned to my new customer, expecting another tourist who wanted a beautiful souvenir to take home. Instead, I came face-to-face with my father. "Father?"

He was in black jeans and a gray t-shirt, an affectionate smile on his lips. "I was in the neighborhood and thought I would stop by." He circled his strong arms around me and placed a kiss on my forehead.

It was nice having this relationship again, to feel happy when I saw my father. I missed his affection, missed how natural things felt between us. "You were not." I pulled away, grinning. "You just stopped by to check on me."

He didn't deny it. "How are you, *tesoro*?"

"I'm okay." A part of me wanted to lie and say I'd never been better, but that lie was too easy to spot. I'd stopped crying all the time, so that was progress. But I didn't mention that to him. "What about you?"

"Good. The house is quiet now that the wedding is over."

"How's Conway?"

He shrugged. "Not sure."

"You haven't spoken to him?" I asked in surprise. Father constantly kept tabs on both of us.

He shook his head. "I'm not calling my son when he's on his honeymoon. We'll talk when he gets back." He turned his gaze to the painting I was photographing. "This is nice."

"Thanks. I have a client who lives in New York. He asked me to take pictures of my new inventory when it comes in. I've started a mailing list, and I'm surprised how many paintings I sell that way."

"That's great, Vanessa." He kept looking at the painting. "I'm very happy to hear that." Sincerity was in his voice, along with fatherly pride.

"Thanks."

"Do you have some time for coffee or lunch?"

I had stuff to do, but my father had come all the way out here, and I wouldn't blow him off. "Yeah. Just let me finish with these pictures so I can send them off. With the time difference—"

"I've got all the time in the world, *tesoro*. Take your time." He drifted away to the other side of the gallery, stopping in front of my painting and examining it with his back turned to me.

I picked up my phone again and resumed the pictures, getting a few good ones with the natural light. Less than a minute later, the front door opened again. I had a few customers throughout the day, but most of them came in after lunchtime. I put my phone in my back pocket and turned around to welcome a prospective client.

But I came face-to-face with Antonio instead.
Shit.

He didn't wear that charming smile he usually had. His eyes were exactly the same as the last time I saw him, focused on me like I was a target he wouldn't allow to escape. In a buttoned-up shirt with the sleeves rolled to his elbows and dark jeans, he looked as handsome as every other time I saw him.

I thought this moment had passed, but I guess it hadn't.

He stopped when he came close to me, and then he stared.

I stared back.

I hated this. I hated this obvious connection. It was impossible to stare at someone like this without it being hostile, but somehow, we made it intimate...when we didn't even know each other. I had the same connection with Bones, and I never wanted to have it with someone else.

But I did.

After a long bout of silence, Antonio spoke. "Have dinner with me." He cut right to the chase, bypassing all the small talk since it seemed pointless. His arms rested by his sides and he kept a few feet between us, but that didn't seem like enough distance. It seemed like we were pressed right up against each other, our lips almost touching.

I stared at him without breathing, unsure how to respond. He didn't even ask me a question, just told me what to do. It didn't seem like he was giving me a choice in the matter. If I'd met this man a year ago, this situation would have unfolded differently. I wouldn't have waited three days to ask him out. I would have asked him then and there. But that wasn't what happened, and I was still in love with the man I'd lost. "I can't."

Antonio didn't react to my rejection. "Why?"

My father was hovering nearby, listening to every word of this conversation. It was bad timing. I didn't know how to answer Antonio without boring him with my life story. I didn't want to get into the details of my heartbreak, not when it still brought me to tears. "I'm not dating right now."

He hadn't blinked once since this conversation began. His stillness suggested he wasn't going anywhere, not until he got what he wanted. "Then I'll wait until you are dating."

I did my best to control my reaction, but I couldn't. Surprise stretched across my face.

"Have coffee with me. As friends."

Even that was too intimate for me, not when I felt this throbbing heat between us. "I can't...I'm sorry." I was the first one to break eye contact, the first one to flinch at the power radiating between us both. My heart was still full of one man, full of the love we shared. Even if we weren't together and we never would be again, Bones was the only man I wanted. To even try to be with someone else right now was futile. And it wouldn't be fair to Antonio, who would have to compete with a man he could never defeat. "It's not gonna happen. You should go..."

He stayed put, his eyes slightly shifting back and forth between mine. He hadn't moved since he'd stopped in front of me. His eyes sped across the surface of my face, flying by at a high velocity. He seemed to be thinking about his next words carefully, how to navigate the intense subject he'd just broached. He probably thought asking me out was going to be simple, just the way it was with all the other woman he picked up and took to bed. He was handsome, artistic, charming, sexy…everything. He never had to lift a finger to get a woman. He never could have anticipated this kind of rejection.

Instead of saying anything else, he turned around and walked out of my gallery. But his silent departure wasn't full of finality. I knew this conversation wasn't over. It was simply paused for the time being.

He would be back.

FATHER and I went to the bakery down the road, the very one I painted.

He got a black coffee and a salad, and I got a cappuccino and a sandwich.

Even though Father heard every word of that conversation, he didn't mention it to me. He sat across from me at the table and sipped his coffee, his eyes directed out the window most of the time.

It was awkward between us since we were both thinking about the same thing at the exact same time. If Antonio had known my father was there, he would have chosen a better time to make his move.

We made small talk about Mama and Conway, but that conversation ran out quickly. Neither one of us participated in the discussion much because our thoughts kept returning to the man who asked me out in the gallery.

Father must have been waiting for me to bring it up, and when I didn't, his patience waned. "Who was the young man?"

I looked down at my cappuccino, seeing the same shade of warm brown in the coffee as I did in Antonio's eyes. "His name is Antonio Tassone. He has a gallery a few blocks down the road. He's an artist as well."

Father drank his coffee, his eyes turning to me. "He paints?"

I nodded.

He didn't ask anything else, hoping I would say more on my own.

"It's a bit ironic…he came into the gallery and bought one of my paintings. About a week later, I went into his gallery and bought one of his…but neither one of us knew they were paintings we'd made. Neither one of us knew we were artists."

He gripped his coffee mug with his fingers. "That's an interesting coincidence."

"Yeah…it is."

"He's a good-looking young man."

I tried not to smile. "I don't think I've ever heard you say anything like that in my life."

"What?"

"Call a man good-looking."

"I'm just saying…" He looked into his coffee and took a drink.

"I'm guessing that's your way of telling me you like him."

He looked out the window and shrugged. "I liked what I saw."

"You don't know anything about him. I don't even know anything about him…"

"But I liked the way he approached you. He was confident, taking control of the conversation and saying what he wanted. When you resisted, he didn't press you. Not only did he not press you, but he said he would wait. He sounds like a gentleman, Vanessa. But a gentleman who's also strong, authoritative, and confident. The fact that you're both artists who enjoy each other's work indicates you're compatible, have a lot in common…and understand one another. Honestly, I don't see a single issue with this man."

"The issue isn't him...and we both know that." I dropped my gaze, unable to look him in the eye once I mentioned Bones.

"Nothing wrong with getting to know someone new."

I didn't want to get to know someone new. "I'm not ready."

"It's been—"

"I'm not ready," I repeated.

My father turned silent.

"I love Griffin as much as I did before. I miss him every day. Getting to know Antonio wouldn't be fair to Antonio. He shouldn't date a woman who's still in love with her ex. And I don't want to force myself to move on from Griffin if I'm not really there. I don't want to rush this. If I rush it, it'll just make it worse."

My father gave a slight nod. "I didn't mean to press you, *tesoro*. I just thought Antonio was a nice young man."

"I'm sure he is..."

Father rested his hand on mine on the table. "I'm sorry."

"It's okay, Father. I'm sorry that happened when you were there."

He pulled his hand away. "It's a little strange to listen to a man ask out your daughter, but I've come to realize you're a grown woman. You're at the time of your life when you're looking to settle down. That's exactly what you should be doing…looking for someone. And I hope you find a great man, a man who loves your artwork as much as you. Because your artwork is a pathway to your soul, and if he understands that…then he understands you."

TEN

Conway

_____

When our honeymoon ended, we drove north from Positano, through Naples, and back toward Florence. The drive was too long to make it in one shot, so we decided to stay with my parents on the journey.

Muse and I spent our time exploring the village, eating lots of pasta, and fucking after dinner. Every day was the same as the previous one, but it felt like a new adventure every time. If she weren't already pregnant, I would have knocked her up by now.

We were thirty minutes from the house when Muse spoke. "Con?"

"Yes, Muse?" I drove with one hand on the wheel, my other hand resting on hers on the center console.

"I love Verona. But…I love it here."

"Where's here?"

"Florence."

I turned to her, still aware of the open road ahead of me. "And what does that mean?"

"Remember when we talked about moving here? To be close to your family?"

"Yes." That was a long time ago.

"Well…how do you feel about it?"

Did it really matter how I felt about it? She was my wife now. She got to call all the shots. "Everything is settled in Verona, including stuff for the baby. My land is there. It's close to work. Moving right now would be an ordeal."

"Moving is always an ordeal…"

"Muse, if you want to move, just tell me."

"No, I want your opinion. Do you want to move?"

I shrugged. "I wouldn't mind being close to family. It would make my parents happy, especially since Vanessa is so close now."

"I love Verona too, but I want to be close to your family—"

"Our family."

She smiled. "Our family. I would love to be close to them. When you're at work, I can always spend time with them with the baby. Vanessa is close by, and she's always been my friend. Carmen is there too, along with your aunt and uncle. If we're going to build a family, I want to be close to family."

It didn't sound like this was a discussion anymore. Muse was asking me to give her what she wanted. When I wasn't around, she wanted some other kind of comfort. She wanted to raise our family with family. In Verona, I was her only companionship.

"I thought you could make a studio here and drive or fly to Milan when you need to…but I know that would make your job less convenient."

Yes, it would be less convenient. But I would be happier knowing my wife was happy. "Let's do it." I turned my eyes to the road, missing her reaction.

She let out a quiet gasp. "Really?"

Hearing the happiness in her voice took away all my doubts. The process of moving everything to a new place would be a lot of work, especially when we had a baby about to join us. Even if we hired people to do it for us, we would still have to sort through everything. But that seemed irrelevant in light of her joy. "Really."

She clapped her hands together. "That makes me so happy. And your parents will be over the moon when they hear the news. All they want is for both you and Vanessa to be close by. Now that Vanessa is down the road, you'll all be together again."

"Yeah. But too bad Vanessa is so down."

"That won't last forever. She's a strong woman. She'll make it through."

"Yeah…" I still hated her depression. It seeped into my skin and penetrated my lungs.

"I can't wait to tell your parents. They'll be so excited."

I remembered the sadness on my mother's face each time I returned to Verona. It broke her heart every single time, made her miserable. Both of my parents wanted the four of us to be united, to be together all the time. I didn't want that when I was younger, but now that I was older, I didn't mind. My father and I had become friends in addition to father and son, and Muse found a good relationship with my mother. "Yeah, they will."

WE GREETED MY PARENTS, talked about the honeymoon, and then had dinner together in the dining room. Lars had prepared a feast that neither one of us needed, but it was so good that we didn't restrain ourselves.

Muse had a much bigger appetite than before, so she always seemed to be hungry.

When I held my wineglass, I felt the bite of the

metal from my wedding ring dig into my skin. I still wasn't used to wearing it, to feeling the metal grow hot and cold with my body temperature. It had a significant weight to it, a weight I still hadn't become accustomed to. Completely black, it would match the color of my suits. My father wore a similar ring, but that wasn't where I drew my inspiration.

"How's Vanessa doing?" I asked.

The happy banter between the four of us died away. Mom's smile faded, and instead, she pressed her lips tightly together in the form of an unhappy grimace. Father looked down into his wine, composing his sentence in his mind before he spoke aloud. "Over-all, she's better. But she's not great."

I wanted Vanessa to get over this guy as soon as possible, not so I wouldn't have to deal with her sadness, but so she would be happy. I didn't like my sister like this, a shell of the person she used to be. So full of life and joy, she was wonderful to be around. She had a spark that could start a forest fire. She had a smile that was brighter than Christmas lights. But all of that faded away once she lost Griffin. "That's too bad…"

"There's this handsome young man who's showed interest in her," Father said. "But she didn't reciprocate his advance."

"Handsome young man?" Both of my eyebrows rose off my face when I heard what my father said. He never talked about potential suitors for Vanessa, and he certainly didn't describe other men like that. He mentioned Muse was a beautiful woman once, but that was the most I'd ever heard him say.

Mom's smile returned. "Your father likes him."

"Wait," Muse said. "Did you meet him?"

"No." Father drank his wine then set it down. "I was in the gallery when it happened. He didn't see me because there was a painting in between us. He walked in and asked her to dinner. He has a gallery down the road. Apparently, he'd come in and bought one of her paintings, unaware that she was the artist who created it. And then she bought one of his, not knowing he was the one who'd made it."

"Really?" I asked. "What are the odds of that?"

"That's what I said," Father said. "They seem perfectly compatible. And when she said she wasn't ready to date, he said he would wait."

"Aww…" Muse's eyes softened.

"And he said he would like to see her as a friend," Father continued. "He was a perfect gentleman, but he wasn't weak either. He's good-looking, confident, and successful. I dug into him after I left and liked everything I saw. He's one of the biggest painters in Italy, and he has galleries all over the world. He's self-made, which I respect."

"He sounds perfect," I said. "I like him already."

Mom shrugged. "But Vanessa doesn't…"

"I don't think that's the case," Father said. "I think she does like him…which is why she doesn't want to see him."

I hated Griffin for coming into our lives. If he hadn't, Vanessa would have met this guy and let him sweep her off her feet. She'd be happy right now, finding her perfect match. But she was still hung up on a criminal.

"She'll figure it out," Mama said. "In her own time. Heartbreak and healing can't be rushed. She's smart for going at her own pace. It's only been two months."

"Only?" I asked incredulously. "That's a long time."

"She was pretty infatuated with Griffin," Mom said. "I'm not surprised. I think she needs another month and then she'll be ready."

I never understood what Vanessa saw in Griffin. They say women have a thing for bad boys. Maybe that was the explanation behind it. "Well, we're over half-way. I want my sister back. I even miss how annoying she used to be…"

Mama smiled, knowing I didn't express my true feelings about Vanessa. "She'll be here soon."

"I miss her too," Father said. "I never expected to have such a strong and brilliant daughter, someone I'm so proud of. She's never put up with bullshit, and she's always understood her self-worth. Independent, smart, and wonderful. I couldn't have asked for anyone better. I can't wait for her to be happy again, and this time, stay happy." Father was never much for words, but whenever he spoke from the heart, it was always poetic.

Mama rested her hand on his on the table. "She will be."

Father moved his fingers in between hers and gripped her hand, his thumb swiping across her soft skin. He gave her an affectionate look, a look he could never hide from us. I saw it all the time when we were growing up. I used to find it repulsive, but now that I was older, seeing my parents still in love made me happy.

It made me want that for myself.

Muse turned to me. "Con, you should tell them the good news."

"What good news?" Mama turned back to us, pulling her gaze off my father reluctantly.

Father looked at me but kept his hand on Mama's. "Tell us."

Muse couldn't stop smiling. Her hair framed her face, and her beautiful eyes were brilliant, pregnant with excitement.

It distracted me for a moment, seeing my wife look so happy. I'd only been married for a few weeks, but I realized all I wanted in life was to keep doing this… making her smile. My priorities had changed after I met her, but now they'd changed again. It was an enormous responsibility, but I took it on without pause.

I felt lucky that the woman I loved adored my family as much as I did. She wore the Barsetti name so effortlessly, had become a part of us since the day she'd met everyone. She wanted to be with them even more than I did, to spend her spare time with my parents and sister when I wasn't around. "We've decided to move here."

Mama's eyes swelled to twice their size, and her mouth popped open with a silent scream. "Really?"

Father didn't react so profoundly. But a smile stretched across his lips, a look of genuine joy. "That's great news."

"You want to raise your family here?" Mama dropped his hand, moving toward Muse anxiously.

"Yes." Muse moved her hand to her stomach. "Verona and Milan are beautiful, but when Conway is at work, I want to be with family. I want our kids to be with family."

Mama's eyes softened in a whole new way, and this time, tears accompanied her expression. "Crow…isn't that wonderful?" She turned back to him, so happy that she looked sad.

He didn't have the same dramatic reaction, but he was definitely happy. "It is. It's what we've always wanted."

"Our babies are back," she whispered. "We can see them all the time."

"Yes, we can." My father wrapped his arm around her and held her, letting her lean on him.

Muse turned to me, a knowing smile on her lips. "I knew they would be happy."

"Yeah." I grabbed her hand on her stomach. "And I know we're going to be happy too."

ELEVEN

Vanessa

Arrangements of geraniums, tulips, and other flowers were right outside the store on a stand. Recently picked and blooming, they were bright with color and vibrant with life. The small shop was several blocks away from my gallery, but I didn't take my car because I enjoyed the walk. I grabbed a coffee on the way and finished it by the time I got there.

When I walked inside, various flowers were scattered across the table, scissors and tools right beside it, along with a thick pair of gloves. Arrangements in glass vases were in the small refrigerator in the back. Directly next to the shop was a little greenhouse, a plot of land that had the perfect location to get sun exposure for most of the day.

Carmen emerged from the back, her hair pulled up

in a loose bun. She wore a yellow sundress, an ideal shade for her olive skin. With bright red lipstick, Barsetti eyes, and a slender figure, she was the perfect person to work in a beautiful shop all day. "Vanessa!" She set down the flowers she was holding and gave me a hug. "What a pleasant surprise. I'm so glad you stopped by."

"The shop looks beautiful. You've made a lot of changes."

"Yeah, I did," she said. "But I like the way it turned out. I wanted something unique, and I think the number of customers has increased because of it."

"Or because of the pretty girl behind the counter," I teased.

She rolled her eyes. "Most of my customers are women."

"They might like the pretty girl behind the counter too."

She chuckled then grabbed the flowers she'd set down, purple tulips. She carried them to the island in the middle of the store. A plastic wrapper was on the table along with some ribbon. "I was just making another arrangement to put outside. I had a whole selection, but it was wiped clean this morning. I'm going to have to find a new place to grow my own flowers. Buying them from someone else is just too expensive, and I'm running out of room."

"Well, both of our parents have a ton of soil."

"No." She dismissed the idea with a shake of her head. "I don't want to use them for anything. I want my business to sustain itself."

"I know what you mean." My family didn't help with my business either. Bones did all of that, his parting gift to me. I stood across from her at the island. "Can I help?"

"Sure." She gave me a pair of shears and some gloves. "Trim all the extra leaves."

"Got it." I started to work.

"I'm surprised you aren't at the gallery."

"I'm on lunch right now. I did a painting this morning, had a few customers, and then closed for an hour. I got a bagel at the coffee shop."

"Some lunch," she teased.

"At least I eat," I countered.

"Whatever," she said with a scoff. "You weren't eating for weeks at one point."

Because I was too depressed. Thinking about that dark time made me falter in my movements.

Carmen immediately looked guilty for what she'd said. "I'm sorry. I didn't mean—"

"It's okay," I said. "Let's just forget it."

She gave me a smile and kept working. "So…rumor has it a hunky man is after you."

I never told her about Antonio, so there was only one way she could have found out. "My father told you?"

"My mama did."

"Which means he told everyone…"

"Naturally," she said. "But don't act surprised. Nothing stays a secret for long with the Barsettis. So why the hell did you say no? That man sounds sexy as sin."

"Because I'm not over Griffin." I shouldn't even have to say that.

"Well, are you ever really going to be over him?" she countered. "That's never going to happen. He's always gonna have a piece of your heart, Vanessa. Even when years pass, you'll never forget him. So maybe the best thing for you to do is move forward."

"Maybe," I said. "But that wouldn't be fair to Antonio. What kind of man wants to be with a woman who's still hung up on her ex? I wouldn't be interested in that…"

"He might not care, Vanessa. He might want you enough to be patient. A really confident man wouldn't care about something like that, because he knows he can make you forget about the other man."

"Not possible." Even if I fell in love again, I would never forget what I had with Bones.

"You never know…" She finished preparing the flowers then arranged them with her fingers. She took the ones I was working on and combined them, placing them in a perfect arrangement because she had a natural ability. "So, you're just going to ignore him forever?"

"I'm not sure what to do."

"Vanessa, he sounds perfect."

I rolled my eyes. "Carmen, I know absolutely nothing about him."

"Not true," she countered. "You know he's a hot painter. What else do you need to know?"

"I'm not sure, but I need more."

"Then get to know him," she countered. "Have coffee with him. You don't have to jump into bed right away. You don't even need to kiss the guy. Just have a conversation."

Having a conversation with him seemed just as intimate as sex, especially when he looked at me like I was the only woman in the world who mattered. "I don't know…"

"Vanessa, you know I liked Griffin. I thought our family was being too harsh and he deserved a better chance. He obviously loved you and was willing to do anything for you. That was all that mattered to me, and I'm sorry our family didn't see it the same way. You should be with him. You should be happy."

I bowed my head, missing him deeply.

"But he's gone, Vanessa. It's over. He's not coming back."

I closed my eyes for a moment, hating the harsh truth.

"So what's the point in staying this way? Staying this miserable? You like this guy, right? Just have coffee with him. That's not scandalous. You aren't betraying Griffin. And you can have coffee with a guy and still be in love with someone else. You could even sleep with him and still be in love with someone else."

"How?" I demanded. "That's wrong."

"Not if you're honest about it," she argued. "Be transparent with him. Tell him exactly what he's getting out of you. He can decide if he still wants to be involved. There's nothing wrong with that."

I looked at the handful of flowers in her hand, surprised by how effortlessly she'd made a professional arrangement. "Those look nice. You're a natural."

"Thanks." She gave me a smile before she dropped it again. "I'll let you change the subject, but think about what I said." She wrapped the plastic around the stems then secured it in place with a rubber band. "Because

there are only so many young, sexy painters out there…
and he's not going to be available for long."

I FINISHED the painting an hour after the sun rose that
morning, so I hung it up in my gallery when it opened.
I'd always been an early riser, and that behavior was
necessary for my artwork. The light couldn't be more
perfect on a clear day, and I captured some of the most
amazing pieces that way.

I wrote the price on the tag before I turned the card
over. It hung on the wall, the other side showing the
name of the painting, along with the date on which I
painted it. I always wrote the exact time it was made on
the bottom corner so people could build a deeper story
around the image. Sometimes they were painted at
sunrise, and sometimes at sunset. Art collectors were
always interested in those things.

"Beautiful." His suave voice and masculine tone
crept up behind me, so smooth his words grazed across
the back of my neck all the way down my spine. My
hair stood on end because of the way his tone
soothed me.

I knew who it was without even turning around. I
kept staring at my painting, my heart suddenly

pounding when I recognized the company I was in. The next step would be to turn around, but I paused for a few more seconds, collecting myself before I faced him head on. I reminded myself that he wasn't as handsome as I imagined, that he was just a man like every other one. He wasn't special, just an artist who shared the same love of artwork. I shouldn't allow him to affect me at all, to make me feel anything.

He waited for me to turn around, patient as always.

I finally turned on the spot, my eyes locking on his. His beard had grown a little thicker, and now hair was sprinkled across his jaw and along his cheeks. Deep brown, nearly black, it complemented his dark skin perfectly. With eyes the color of warm coffee on a winter day, he was even more beautiful than I remembered. In a black V-neck and black jeans, he looked handsome as hell in the color. It matched his dark hair and eyes.

Damn.

His lips rose softly in a smile, his mood elevating the longer he looked at me. Antonio seemed to read my moods, to understand what I was thinking even though he didn't know me well enough to do so.

"Thank you." I forced the words out, choosing to speak instead of sit in silence. The silence was worse than talking because it was too intense, too potent. "I painted it this morning."

His soft smile remained, but his eyes focused further on my face. His eyebrows shifted slightly. "I wasn't talking about the painting."

Shit.

"But it's beautiful as well."

My hair was down today, one of the first times I'd actually done anything with it. But I skipped the makeup and the cute outfit. I wore a light blue summer dress and sandals since it was going to be a hot day in the city. When it was humid and warm, jeans were a terrible choice. My skin had started to deepen in color from being in the sun more often, so the tone contrasted with the brightness of my dress.

I knew Antonio wasn't going to walk away from me, not so easily. He'd left me alone for the past few days, just like last time. He seemed to have a pattern, or it was just a coincidence.

My eyes shifted to the floor, breaking the contact because I couldn't take it anymore. With Bones, I could hold his gaze forever without flinching. When he made love to me, I never stopped staring at him, even when our lips touched. Looking at Antonio made me think of those nights, and the idea of having that kind of intimacy with him terrified me.

"Don't be afraid to look at me."

"I'm not." I flicked my eyes up again, remembering I should never back down. "I just don't want to."

Again, the rejection didn't sting him the way it would sting someone else. It was like he didn't hear it at all, like it didn't mean anything. He seemed to see past my excuses and my lies to the truth behind them.

That I felt exactly what he felt.

"There's so much beauty in the truth. So let's only speak with the truth."

It was a riddle of a sentence, but I somehow grasped his meaning. "I told you I wasn't interested."

"I remember." He kept his arms by his sides, his muscled arms covered in veins the way I liked. His skin was beautiful, kissable. A corded vein went up his neck, prominent against his tight skin. Without his having to remove his shirt, it was clear to see that he was ripped in all the right places. There was nothing but muscle underneath that cotton. "But it wasn't the truth."

"I'm not ready to see anyone."

"I believe that one," he said. "And I respect it."

"Doesn't seem like it." I crossed my arms over my chest.

He watched my movements before his eyes flicked back to mine. "I'm only asking for your companionship, nothing else. Have dinner with me. Let's get some coffee or gelato. Whatever you want. All I'm asking for is your time. Please give it to me."

We bypassed all the normal conversation that two strangers had. We skipped to the middle, speaking to each other with such candidness it was like we'd known each other our entire lives. The connection was so strong there was nothing I could do to stop it. It was there—and we both knew it. "I don't want to waste your time. You're a beautiful man…there's not a woman out there you couldn't have."

He raised one eyebrow, sincerely surprised. "Even if that were true, I don't want a woman out there. Right now, I want the woman in here. And you've never wasted my time, Vanessa. Even when you reject me, I still enjoy these moments."

The way he said my name sent shivers down my spine. It was intimate, like he pressed his lips against mine and said my name directly into my throat. "I'm in love with another man…" I said the words out loud and felt a jolt of pain in my chest. I didn't want to hurt Antonio, and I didn't want to harbor these feelings any longer. Carmen made an excellent point when I spoke to her that afternoon. Carrying a vigil for Bones in my heart hadn't done me any good. It only caused me pain.

Again, Antonio didn't react. It was like those words

meant nothing to him. "But you aren't seeing him anymore."

"How did you know…?"

"Because if you really were with someone else…" He raised his hand and moved it toward me before he pointed at his chest. "Then this wouldn't be happening. So this man must be gone…either from life or your life."

"Yes…he is."

He lowered his hand again. "I appreciate your bluntness. But it doesn't change anything."

This man was so confident that he didn't care what I'd just said. It didn't seem like he was concerned about anything I could say. He wanted me, and he wasn't going to stop until he had me. "I'm just not ready. It wouldn't be fair to date someone when I still feel this way. When I put myself out there again, I want to be ready to love someone. I'm definitely not there, and that's not fair to you, to anyone."

He gave a slight nod. "I understand your reasoning. The timing isn't right. Ordinarily, I wouldn't be interested in getting involved with someone under those circumstances. But I want to get to know you anyway. All I'm asking for is your friendship. That's something you should be able to give me right now."

"I…"

"Vanessa." His voice sounded a little more powerful when he spoke my name, the word reverberating off the walls of my gallery. It went straight into my ear, making me melt into a puddle on the floor. "Have coffee with me." This time, it didn't sound like a request but a command.

"I just…" I couldn't keep denying him forever. He would find his way into my heart eventually. At least I could do this on my terms. "Alright. But I want something from you, a promise."

His shoulders tightened slightly when I said yes. "Anything."

"Don't kiss me." I didn't want him to walk me to my door and surprise me with an embrace. I didn't want him to slide his hand into my hair and caress me with his mouth. I didn't want him to rush the relationship, not when I wasn't ready for it.

His eyes didn't flash with disappointment or annoyance. "How about this. Anytime I want to kiss you, I'll tell you. If you don't want me to, say nothing. And when you are ready, just say yes."

That still gave me the power to stop anything physical from happening, and I also didn't actually have to say a word to enforce it. Antonio seemed like a man who would keep his word, and if he didn't, he knew I would never trust him. So it seemed like this was going to work. "Okay."

That handsome smile stretched across his lips, making his brown eyes shine a little brighter. He looked at me with possession, like he'd finally gotten what he wanted. "I'll pick you up after work."

IT WAS a quiet evening in the coffee shop. Most of the tables were empty, and the sound of the gentle music overhead was low. The glass counter was stuffed with different pastries, and the workers used the large espresso machine to make steaming cups of coffee.

I sat at the table with my foamy cappuccino in front of me, froth on top along with sprinkled chocolate. It was a short cup on top of a saucer with a small handle.

Antonio got a black coffee—keeping it simple.

I hadn't taken a drink yet because the drink was too hot.

Antonio watched me from across the table, wearing a white linen collared shirt with the sleeves rolled to his elbows. The stark color was perfect on him, contrasting against his dark skin and hair. His eyes matched my coffee, warm and smooth.

I tilted my face down and took a drink, letting the froth move over my tongue and down my throat.

Antonio kept his fingers around his mug but didn't take a drink. He seemed far more fascinated with me than anything else in that café.

I thought we'd come here to talk, but all we seemed to do was stare. It was the strangest first date I'd ever been on. When I met guys on the town, we usually flirted back and forth, made small talk, and if there was a spark there, I saw them again. But in this instance, talking was unnecessary. We seemed to like each other without really knowing one another. "How long have you had your gallery?"

"Ten years," he answered. "I also have one in Milan and Positano, along with a few outside the country. But I've settled in Florence for the foreseeable future. It's a great city. I can get the chaos of the city and then drive a few miles and be in the countryside."

"You live in town?"

"Yes. I live a few blocks from the shop in an apartment. If I lived above my shop like you do, I would never stop working." He gave me a smile before he took a drink of his coffee.

That was all I ever did with my time—work. "My world seems to revolve around it."

"That's how you know you're an artist, when it's all you ever want to do."

I took another drink of my cappuccino, letting the froth stick to my lips. I licked it away with my tongue.

Antonio watched me, his eyes glued to my mouth. His gaze narrowed slightly, his focus pinpointed on that spot of my anatomy. He forced his gaze back to my eyes again, but there were remnants of his attraction. "I didn't recognize your last name right away. But are you associated with Barsetti Vineyards?"

"Yes. My parents and uncle run a few in Tuscany."

He nodded. "Great wine. I've got at least two bottles at home."

"Thanks. When I first got started, I would hang my paintings at the winery. Customers would buy them when they were wine tasting."

His eyes brightened in approval. "Smart idea. Most people who wine taste are tourists, so they usually want a souvenir to take home. What an excellent marketing strategy. That seems to be the biggest hardship for artists, finding a place to show their work. Selling your stuff on a street corner doesn't exactly project quality artwork."

"Exactly."

"And then you opened this shop a few months ago?"

"Yeah…" I had nothing to do with it. Bones made the leap for me. He believed in me so much that he laid the foundation for my future for me. He got me a great gallery, a great apartment, and a car. He established the rest of my life, giving me the independence I'd always wanted.

Antonio seemed to catch my look of sadness because it mirrored my own. "Where were you before this?"

I decided to skip my time in the countryside with Bones. It didn't seem like a story I could appropriately slip into the conversation. "I was actually going to university in Milan. I was studying fine art."

"Did you graduate?"

"No…I dropped out."

He grinned, like that impressed him. "You made the right decision. There was nothing more you needed to learn."

It was a quite a compliment coming from someone like him, a man who'd made a living as an artist for over a decade. When I looked into his work, I saw his expert craftsmanship. He was brilliant with the paint-brush, constructing beauty from just his mind.

"There are techniques we all need to learn, but art isn't something that can be taught. It's something that you're born with, something that you feel. Paying someone to teach their opinion on the matter isn't the best way to spend your time. You should spend your time painting—only painting."

"Yeah. I think I made the right decision."

"Yes. You did."

"What about you?" I asked. "How did it happen for you?" Now that the conversation was going, I didn't feel so uncomfortable being this close to him. It seemed to feel natural. A relationship based on more than deep attraction and connection began to form.

"I'd always known I wanted to be a painter from a young age. I was a teenager when I got serious about it. By the time I was an adult, I'd sold a few paintings. Things fell into place then, and I never looked back. I started my own gallery when I was twenty, took out a loan from the bank, and once I found success, I kept going. It's been a great ten years."

"Wow...that's amazing. Your family must be proud."

"My mother always was. My father was angry about it for a long time. He's a businessman, operating a few restaurants. He wanted me to get into business or finance, something steady. He never thought I wasn't good enough to be an artist, but he didn't think it was appropriate to pursue. But once I opened my third shop and proved my success, he finally came around."

My parents would never act that way. Whatever I wanted to do, they would always be supportive. When Conway wanted to be a lingerie designer, they were supportive of that too. There was nothing we could do or say to make them disapprove of us. Then I remembered the one thing they could never accept…the one person they could never approve. It was the only instance when my parents didn't give me what I wanted. It was too difficult for them to look past. "You proved him wrong a million times over…"

He nodded, still smiling. "Yeah, I did. And it felt good." His collared shirt fit across his chest nicely, stretching over the muscles of his upper body. He was lean, but it was clear he was strong. I'd seen his sculpted arms before, and it seemed like everything else under his linen shirt was the same. "Can I ask you about the painting you bought from me?"

I had it hanging in my living room, a perfect picture of Tuscany. I could talk about artwork forever, so the question didn't bother me. "Of course."

"What made you love it so much? Don't worry, my ego isn't fishing for compliments. But, you know, one or two wouldn't hurt."

He made me smile against my will. Even a small chuckle escaped my chest. "I really loved the colors. It was painted in the morning, right?"

He nodded. "Yes."

"I grew up in Tuscany, spending my time at the winery with my parents and looking out my bedroom window to the vineyards beyond. Whether it's sunrise or sunset, the place is so beautiful. It's so simple. When I looked at your painting, my childhood flashed before my eyes. I'd painted a similar image many times, but your work spoke to my heart. I had to hang it in my living room. I had to see it every single day."

His smile faded away, a softness in his eyes. "That's quite a compliment."

"You're quite an artist."

"Never realized how much until right now. It's one thing to create something that someone loves, but it's another to capture something that someone has experienced a hundred times…but it somehow makes them feel something new. That's the purpose of art, to make people feel something when they look at it. That's what I love about my work, and hearing you say all those things…makes me very happy."

When he was touched, he had this warm look in his eyes. He was so talented but so humble at the same time. He seemed to care about the success of his artwork, not of himself personally. He was deeply artistic, poetic, and sensitive. Well-spoken and well-read, he was a special kind of man. I'd never met anyone like him before. "May I ask why you liked mine?"

His expression became focused once more. "Yes. I was hoping you would. I loved all the details in it, from the scrapes against the limestone wall, to the flower boxes full of geraniums, to the old, beat-up blue bicycle parked in the alleyway, to the slightly slanted window that we're sitting in front of now. It was a better image than any camera could capture. The vibrant red color of the flowers in contrast to the ancient brown stone. It illustrated a small moment in Florence, a moment I'd experienced so many times. Unlike a photograph, it was so much more evocative…so much more emotional. When you're painting something, you're capturing a feeling, an emotion, and you did a beautiful job of accomplishing that."

Hearing such heartfelt praise over something I cared so much about meant the world to me. When Bones loved my artwork, it pulled at my heartstrings. It made me fall for him, because even though he knew nothing about art, he felt something. Now I was listening to a professional praise my work, and his words weren't empty because he'd bought my painting before he even knew anything about me. Everything he said was sincere. "Thank you…that means a lot coming from you."

"Why?" He cocked his head slightly to the side.

"Because you're an amazing artist."

He chuckled quietly. "As flattered as I am, I have to correct you. I think your talent far exceeds mine. The only difference between us is I've been in the game much longer. When I buy artwork, I'm very picky. There's only so much wall space, and you have to choose carefully. I never want to throw a painting away. I have collections ranging from Monet to Picasso. When I saw yours, I didn't think twice about it. I knew I had to have it. So before you assume I'm the better artist, just keep that in mind."

GETTING coffee with Antonio was much better than I expected. The conversation unfolded naturally, and by the end, it seemed like I was getting coffee with an old friend. He was interesting, polite, and easy on the eyes. He never made it seem like a date. When we'd first walked into the coffee shop, he didn't even try to pay for my drink.

It was nice.

I enjoyed his company because we had so much in common, and it was nice to talk to someone who had no tie to my past. With Antonio, I didn't have to see him pity me like the rest of my family did. It felt like a fresh start, turning over a new leaf. He was the first friend I'd made in Florence, and I hoped he would stay my friend.

We left the coffee shop and walked back to my apartment, his arm almost touching my shoulder on the sidewalk. The streetlamps were on, and there were very few people passing through town. I was only a few blocks away, and even though I told him I could make it back on my own, he insisted on escorting me.

"Thanks for having coffee with me," he said. "I enjoyed getting to know you better, Vanessa."

I loved it when he said my name. He had such a sexy voice, and he made the single word sound so deep. "Yeah…I did too."

He stopped in front of my gallery, next to the stairs that led to the second story where my apartment was located. He didn't try to walk me right to the door, which was a relief. We stood on the sidewalk, in the glow of the light from the streetlamp. There weren't any pedestrians near us, so it seemed like we were completely alone.

I faced him, purposely keeping several feet between us. "Well…goodnight."

He kept his hands in his pockets. "Goodnight." He

stayed rooted to the spot, looking at me with chocolate-colored eyes.

I'd already said goodnight, but I was still standing there.

He smiled slightly.

"What?"

"Nothing," he said, still wearing that charming grin. "I knew we would have a good time if you just gave me a chance."

"Well, it's nice to make a new friend." I purposely dropped that word in there, rejecting him subtly. I didn't mean to offend him, but I didn't want him to think anything had changed between us. I enjoyed his company and he enjoyed mine, and if this had been a real date, I'd be inviting him to my apartment right now. But my heart was still in the same place as it was before…in the palm of a different man.

Like always, Antonio wasn't offended by the way I turned him down. "Absolutely." He took a step closer to me, closing the gap in between us until we were dangerously close.

I stopped breathing for a second, my heart pounding at the proximity.

His eyes shifted down to look at me since he was so much taller than me. He had a kind face, but he also had a sexy smolder without trying. He stood perfectly straight like a confident man, understanding the exact effect he had on me.

He said he wouldn't kiss me unless I asked, so I knew there was nothing to be afraid of. I could tell he was a man who kept his word, and it didn't seem like something he would do so soon anyway.

"I think a handshake would be strange. So, how about a hug?" He kept his hands in his pockets, not touching me with his fingers but touching me with his proximity. His soft eyes looked into mine, commanding my full attention. His piercing gaze burned me from the inside out, made me feel alive.

I stared at him.

He waited for a yes, and if he didn't get it, he wouldn't touch me.

I didn't see anything wrong with a hug. Friends shared more affection than that on a daily basis. "Sure."

The corner of his mouth rose in a smile before he moved in. His arms circled my waist, his large palms gliding across my back. He pulled me into him, making my tits hit his strong chest. Instead of moving his face into my neck, he rested his forehead right against mine.

My arms circled around his neck, and I froze as I sucked in a deep breath. I hadn't expected the intimate closeness, the feel of his breath on my face. I expected a quick hug, something that wouldn't last longer than five seconds.

But it seemed to go on forever.

He held me outside my apartment, his large hands taking up most of my back. His cologne was heavy, along with a hint of paint. With his fingertip touched the bare skin between my shoulder blades, I couldn't contain the air in my lungs. I took a deep breath, moved by the touch.

He kept his forehead against mine, his eyes closed. He never moved in to kiss me, keeping his distance like he promised.

All I had to do was move out of the way, and he would let me go. But I stayed there. I stayed absolutely still, like any movement would bring him closer or push him farther away. My hands moved down his arms, feeling the solid muscle I'd stared at in the past. I rested my palms on the crook of his elbows, feeling the prominent veins underneath his skin.

A quiet moan escaped his throat, just as his chest rose and fell with a deep breath. "Fuck…"

I imagined him saying that very word in bed, when he was hot and sweaty on top of me, enjoying me. I loved being touched by someone, getting affection I hadn't had in so long. The last few days with Bones were full of tears and heartbreak, not real connection.

The sex wasn't what it used to be, not when all we could think about was saying goodbye. I didn't realize how much I wanted it until now, from a man that wasn't Bones.

"I could do this forever."

I could do this forever too, and that's what scared me. I liked everything about Antonio, from his personality to his confidence. I liked the way he carried himself, the way he created art. I liked the connection we had, as if we'd known each other before we even met. But those feelings alarmed me, made me feel so much guilt that I despised myself. It's been months since Bones left and he'd been with other women by now, but that didn't change the way I felt. I stepped back, putting an end to the tenderness before I could enjoy it a second longer. "I should get going…" I turned my back on him before he even had the opportunity to say anything.

His footsteps sounded as he followed me to the stairs. "Vanessa."

I stepped on the first stair and gripped the rail.

He spoke again, a little more authoritatively. "Vanessa." He didn't reach out and grab me, but his voice was enough.

I turned around, eye level with him.

"How long has it been?" He moved his hands into

his pockets again, telling me he wouldn't try to touch me.

I knew he was asking about the man I loved. "Two months."

"That's a long time."

"Not long enough," I whispered. "I'm sorry. I told you I wasn't ready——"

He held up his hand to silence me. "You don't owe me an apology or an explanation. I'm only asking."

I gripped the rails on either side of me.

He returned his hand to his pocket. "Can I ask what happened?"

"I…I don't know."

He nodded to the steps. "Sit with me."

After a moment of hesitation, I sat on the bottom step with him. There were a few inches between us, so we weren't touching.

He rested his arms on his knees, his hands coming together. "Did he pass away?"

"No. I'll give you the short version of the long version…"

"The long version is fine with me." He stared straight ahead, looking at the street.

"My family has a long history with his family. His father did some terrible things to my mother and aunt. That was before I was even born. Then I met Griffin…

the son of the man who did all those terrible things. I didn't expect to fall in love with him. I did my best not to. I even hated him like everyone else at one point… but I couldn't help it. I fell in love with him. We were really happy together. I didn't want to keep it a secret forever, so we tried to get my family to accept him. But that didn't work. My father tried to get to know him and let go of the past, but eventually, he just couldn't do it. He told me he didn't want me to see Griffin anymore. I know I'm a grown woman who doesn't have to listen to my parents, but my family is so close that I need a husband who can be part of my family. I want a husband whom my father will love like a son. That wasn't him…so we went our separate ways. That was almost two months ago…"

He massaged his knuckles, listening to every word I'd said. "I'm sorry to hear that."

"You are?" I whispered.

He nodded. "He's your first love?"

"And my only love."

"Then, yes, I'm sorry to hear that. It's rough losing someone you love."

"It is."

"So, you feel guilty for having feelings for me… because you feel like you're betraying him."

"I never said I have feelings for you."

A long stretch of silence passed. "You've never needed to. I can feel it, Vanessa. I can feel this connection between us. The second I realized we fell in love with each other's paintings, I knew there was something special here. It's not just physical or romantic…but something else. I'm not the kind of guy that goes after women who are heartbroken over someone else. I'm not that patient. But with you…I realized I could be as patient as necessary."

"You hardly know me."

"I know," he said. "And I have the rest of time to get to know you…which I'm looking forward to."

"It's hard for me to imagine myself being with anyone else. I thought I would marry Griffin. I still miss Griffin."

"It takes time. And I don't mind waiting for as long as that takes…as your friend. When I held you, I felt this explosion inside my chest. Sex has never felt that good. Love has never felt that good. But whatever that was…it felt right."

I felt it too, but I refused to admit it out loud.

"I will gladly settle for being your friend until you're ready to be something more."

"I don't know how long that will be, Antonio. You shouldn't waste your time on me. There could be someone much better out there."

"I doubt it," he whispered. "There are a lot of beautiful women in the world. All special in their own way, they're smart, interesting, fun…everything. But I've never felt this way for any of them. I was never looking for something serious. I was never looking to settle down. And then one interaction with you changed all of that. You know exactly what I'm talking about…I can feel it. But you aren't ready to acknowledge it or embrace it. That's fine. I would rather wait until you are…because when you're ready, I want all of you. I don't want just a piece of you."

I stared forward, unsure what to say to that deep confession. Antonio was mature, poetic, and unbelievably romantic. If only this had happened some other time, I might have said I found the person I wanted to spend my life with. I would have been swept off my feet, and we would be making love all night long right upstairs. If I'd met Antonio first, Bones might never have had a chance.

But I did meet Bones first. And he was the man I loved. "We'll see what happens. But for right now, at this moment in time, we're friends. Just friends."

A WEEK PASSED, and I didn't see Antonio. He seemed

to give me the space I needed, the space I never asked for. Our galleries were so close together, but we never crossed paths. I was sure he made that intentional, knowing I couldn't be with him all the time. If we really were just friends, then there was no reason to see each other on a daily basis.

That embrace we shared in front of my apartment gave me a rush of feelings. It felt good. I would go as far as to say it felt right. But at the same time, my heart rejected the affection because it was too soon. I hadn't healed yet. I still needed more time.

I was in the gallery when my family surprised me. Conway and Sapphire stopped by, along with Carmen.

"Wow, it looks so nice in here," Sapphire said. "You've got paintings on every wall, and they're all new."

"I make a few paintings every week to keep the walls stocked," I said. "I've actually been selling paintings pretty consistently. I started an email list, so old clients come back and buy new paintings. I just ship them out."

"That's awesome," Conway said. "It sounds like your gallery is a success."

"Yeah, it is." Thanks to one special person who made all of this possible. My father could have done the same for me, but I never would have accepted it.

He'd done so much for me already. "How was the honeymoon?"

"Beautiful," Sapphire said with excitement. "I loved it there. We were right by the harbor with all the ships…and the food…I could go on and on about the food."

"Pregnancy will do that to you," Carmen said. "I can't wait to be pregnant."

"You hardly eat as it is," I countered.

"But when you're pregnant, you can get away with it," Carmen said. "And people think it's cute."

"I think my wife is cute no matter what she does," Conway said, his eyes on Sapphire.

Carmen and I both made a disgusted face.

Sapphire beamed brighter than before.

"Anyway," I said. "Did you guys just stop by? Or did you want to get lunch?"

"Yes," Carmen said. "You have an hour to spare?"

"Of course," I said. "The shop can close for an hour."

We left the gallery and walked up the road.

"Maybe you should hire someone," Conway suggested. "Someone who can run the gallery while you aren't there. You could spend that time painting."

"Maybe," I said. "I've only been in business for a few months, so I wanted it just to be me for a while. But pretty soon, I may need the help. So, where did you want to go?"

"How about that bakery over here?" Carmen said. "They've got good sandwiches."

There was a slight hint of anxiety in my chest since that was Antonio's favorite place. I didn't want to run into him, not when my family was in tow.

"Let's go," Sapphire said. "I could go for a turkey sandwich and a decaf."

"Whatever my muse wants," Conway said, not really caring.

Looked like I was outnumbered even if I wanted to make a protest. "Sounds good to me." We walked inside and ordered, and of course, my billionaire brother had to be the big shot and pay the bill.

We sat at a table near the window with our coffees and lunch and talked about the wedding and the honeymoon. My brother seemed happy with Sapphire, even happier than he was before. He was different before she came along, a lot quieter and brooding. All he cared about was money, success, and booze. But once the jewel of his life came along, his priorities changed. He showed a more vulnerable side that I liked to see. Even if I hadn't liked Sapphire personally, I would love her because she made my brother better. But fortunately, she was an awesome sister to have.

"What's new with you?" Sapphire asked me. "Besides the gallery."

All three of them looked at me, wanting me to talk about Antonio. They all knew about him because my father couldn't keep his damn mouth shut. "Nothing, really. I sold a few paintings this week. It's been a pretty hot summer, so I've been eating a lot of gelato."

They all wore a look of annoyance, wanting me to discuss the elephant in the room.

But I refused to mention Antonio, not when he was just a friend and nothing more. I drank my coffee and kept my eyes on my food.

Conway stared at me but didn't press me on it.

Carmen practically exploded because she'd been holding her breath for so long. "What about Antonio? Have you seen him since?"

I rolled my eyes. "Shut up, Carmen."

"Oh, come on," she said. "We're all thinking about him, so you might as well spill it."

"There's nothing to say," I said. "He's just my friend."

"Her apparently *hot* friend," Carmen said to Sapphire. "If he didn't already have a thing for her, I'd be swooping in…"

"Then swoop in," I said. "You can have him."

Carmen laughed sarcastically. "That would drive you crazy, and you know it. You like the guy."

"I don't want to talk about this, alright?" I said. "He's just a—" I almost dropped my coffee when Antonio walked inside, dressed in jeans that hung low on his hips and a t-shirt that made his arms look incredible. His chiseled jaw was as sexy as ever, and I remembered exactly how those big arms felt wrapped around me. I remembered the heat between us when he held me close. I remembered losing my breath because the chemistry was so scorching. My body naturally hummed to life when I looked at him because I found him deeply attractive, his mind and his body.

When I stopped talking, Carmen's eyes drifted to him. "Look who it is…"

Shit. I hoped he wouldn't see me, but the place was so small, it was only a matter of time before he spotted me.

Carmen raised her hand. "Antonio!"

You've got to be kidding me. "Carmen!"

"What?" she asked innocently. "Can't say hi to your *friend*?"

Why was this happening to me?

Antonio stopped when he heard his name, and once his eyes took me in, he changed his direction and came my way, grinning in his typically charming way.

Conway immediately watched him, examining him like a protective older brother. He'd never liked Bones, could barely say two words to him. He wouldn't like anyone, because in his eyes, no one was ever good enough for me.

Antonio was about to walk into a trap.

Confident as ever, he approached me and three strangers. He greeted me before he spoke to anyone else. "Vanessa, how are you?"

"I'm good…" I could have come up with something better than that, but words failed me when I needed them the most.

He patiently waited for me to introduce him to everyone, and when that didn't happen, he did it himself. "Allow me to introduce myself. Antonio." He extended his hand to Carmen first. "Family? You have the same features."

"Carmen," she said. "And yes, we're cousins."

He turned to Sapphire next. "Nice to meet you."

"Sapphire," she said. "This is my husband, Conway." She smiled when she said the word husband, grinning from ear to ear.

Antonio extended his hand.

I expected Conway not to take it, to grill him with a million questions. But instead, my brother stood up and shook his hand.

I couldn't believe what I was seeing.

"Nice to meet you." Conway gave him a firm grip and looked him in the eye. "How about you join us for lunch?"

My mouth dropped open. "Seriously?"

Antonio and Conway both turned to me at the same time. Conway glared at me, and Antonio seemed genuinely bewildered.

"You're just going to invite him to eat with us when you know nothing about him?" I asked in shock. "You don't know anything about this guy. He could be a rapist or something."

Antonio lowered his hand, and instead of being offended, he smiled. "Uh…I'm not a rapist. Just so everyone knows…"

Conway continued to glare at me. "Knock it off, Vanessa. I'd like to meet your friend."

"You've never cared about any of my other friends before," I snapped. "You never made an effort—"

"Vanessa, be quiet." Conway threatened me with his hostile gaze. "You're overreacting."

The only reason why my brother was being so polite was because he wanted me to forget about Bones. But if Antonio were just some random guy, Conway would have growled at him like a watchdog. He wanted

Bones to be a distant memory so much that he didn't care who showed an interest in me.

Antonio picked up on the tension. "I'm going to grab a coffee. I'll be right back." He headed to the counter so we could talk in private.

Conway sat down again, his wedding ring standing out because he'd never worn jewelry before he got married. He kept his voice low so no one would overhear us. "If you don't want to die alone, I suggest you knock it off. Antonio seems like a nice guy, and I'd like to get to know him."

"Because Father liked his ten-second interaction with him?" I asked incredulously.

"No," Conway said with seriousness. "Because this guy doesn't kill anyone. That's why I like him. Griffin set the bar pretty damn low."

I took a deep breath, insulted by the remark. "And you're so much better? I'm sure Sapphire loved being a prisoner for—"

"Don't go there." He looked like he wanted to flip the table over. "I've been patient with you because you're going through a hard time. I love you, so I've been pretty damn understanding. I hate seeing you in pain. I hate the rubble Griffin left behind. But my patience is worn out, Vanessa. I'm sick of your dramatic bullshit, and I'm not putting up with it anymore. The whole reason we're here is to check on you. Don't forget that Father is the one who made the decision, not me. I could be doing anything else right now, but I'm here with you—as are all of us. So instead of pushing us away and making an idiot out of yourself in front of this guy, chill the fuck out."

Just when he finished his sentence, Antonio came to our table with a mug in his hand. "So, is that invitation still on the table?" He stood next to the chair, not crossing the line I'd drawn on the floor.

Conway stared at me, still pissed.

Antonio looked at me, his warm eyes full of patience.

I didn't want to be angry with my brother, not when he'd always been there for me. And I didn't want to make Antonio feel unwelcome, not when he'd always been so kind to me. It wasn't his fault that I actually liked him. "Yes." I finally looked him in the eye. "Please join us."

He smiled slightly before his eyes lit up with approval. "I'd love to." He sat down and set his cup on the table, keeping his posture perfectly straight and his shoulders squared. Steam wafted from his coffee toward the ceiling. He looked at me for a moment longer, quickly reading the expression on my face before he turned to my family. "I bought one of Vanessa's paintings. It's hanging in my apartment right now, in the living room. She's very talented. I'm sure you guys already know that…but she is."

Carmen grinned from ear to ear as she listened to him talk, affected by his sexy voice just the way I was. "She is. We're all so impressed by her. No one else inherited this talent."

Conway cleared his throat.

"You aren't a painter," Carmen said.

"You design lingerie, right?" Antonio asked. "I love painting, but I think you might have the best job in the world." He wore a playful grin, indicating he was joking.

Conway obviously liked the compliment. "There are worse ways to make a living. And it's how I met my wife." He moved his arm around her shoulders.

"That's awesome," Antonio said. "And you've got a little one on the way?"

"Yes." Sapphire moved her hand to her stomach. "They'll be here in a few months."

"Congratulations." Antonio turned back to me. "You're about to be an aunt. Very exciting."

"Are you an uncle yet?" Conway asked. It was shocking my brother was asking him anything considering he hated seeing me with a man at any time. He usually intervened in my dates, didn't aid in them. But now he was talking to Antonio like a friend, making him feel welcome instead of barking at him like a guard dog.

"Yes." Antonio drank from his mug. "I have two nieces."

"Aw, that's nice…" I was learning this information for the first time. It was strange that I didn't know Antonio at all but I enjoyed his company so deeply. I was comfortable around him even though there was no foundation to our friendship. We just clicked. "How old are they?"

He turned back to me, clearly excited by my interest. "Seven and four. They're beautiful little girls—like my sister. But don't tell her I said that. She's got a huge ego."

I chuckled. "Your secret is safe with me." It reminded me of something Conway would say in confidence, before my parents stabbed him in the back and told me what he said.

"Does everyone live in Florence?" Antonio asked.

"No." Conway rubbed the back of Sapphire's neck. "My wife and I live in Verona. But we actually have some exciting news…" He turned his gaze to me.

I already knew what he was going to say before he said. "You're serious? You guys are moving back to Tuscany?"

Sapphire couldn't keep the words in her throat. "Yes! We're looking for a house right now."

"What?" Carmen almost knocked over her coffee mug when she threw her arms down. "That's so awesome! Do your mom and dad know?"

"Yes," Conway answered. "We told them last week."

"You have no idea how happy you just made them." My parents were hurt that I was heartbroken, but they were also happy I was right down the road. Both of my parents stopped by to see me whenever they felt like it, and they were overjoyed to have my close by. Now their son was back in town, just when he was starting his family.

"I think we do," Conway said confidently. "So, it looks like the two of us will be seeing a lot more of each other."

"Good." My brother could be a jackass sometimes, but it didn't change the love I had for him. "I miss seeing both of you. Now Sapphire and I can hang out all the time, bringing the baby along."

"We can have those family dinners every week," Carmen said. "It feels like our family just got a little bigger."

I felt Antonio stare at me, so I shifted my gaze to him. He wore a gentle smile, his eyes lit up with affection. His thoughts were clearly written on his face, his adoration for me obvious in the glow of his coffee eyes.

"What?" I asked.

He grinned before he looked down at his coffee again. "You're cute, that's all." He said the words out loud, not caring that my brother and cousin heard it. His confidence always dictated his behavior, made him indifferent to the opinion of others. He didn't care what anyone thought of him, and that made him even sexier. "I like a woman who's close with her family. I'm exactly the same way."

ANTONIO RETURNED TO WORK, and the four of us walked back to my gallery to say goodbye. Carmen had to return to her shop, and Conway and Sapphire were having dinner with my parents.

"Thanks for coming down to see me," I said, appreciating the fact that I was never alone, even in my darkest hour. My brother was always there for me, even when I didn't deserve it. I looked up to him in ways he would never understand.

"Of course." Conway gave me a one-armed hug. "It's nice to see that you're doing better."

"I am?" I asked in surprise.

"Definitely." Sapphire hugged me next. "It's the first time I've seen you smile in over two months."

I smiled? "Yeah…I guess so."

Conway kept his arm around Sapphire's waist as he looked at me on the sidewalk. "I like Antonio."

I didn't narrow my eyes even though I wanted to. "Con, you hardly know him."

"But I liked what I saw," he said. "He included himself in our conversation instead of being intimidated. He connected with all of us. He made jokes, never took himself too seriously, and he was always himself. Plus, I can tell he's hung up on you."

I tried to stop the blush from entering my cheeks, but it was no use.

"So infatuated with you," Sapphire said. "It's obvious."

They had no idea just how intimate Antonio and I had already been, that he was willing to wait until I was ready before something could finally happen between us. The second he set his sights on me, he'd made up his mind.

"Any man who can spend time with your family so casually is good enough," Conway said. "Father looked into him and saw how successful this guy is. Now I've seen how down-to-earth he is. This guy has nothing to hide. He's clean and kind. That's all we want, someone who understands you and can make you happy."

"As much as I appreciate that, you're still jumping the gun," I said. "I'm not dating Antonio. We're just friends. I'm not ready to be in another relationship. I'm not even ready to go on a date."

"That's fine," Conway said. "And it's obvious this guy likes you enough to be patient with you. But whenever you are ready, he's got the approval of the whole family, which is something you've always wanted in a partner. So…just keep that in mind."

TWELVE

Vanessa

────────────

Weeks passed, and during that time, I focused on my painting and running the gallery. Business picked up so much that I considered hiring someone to help me run the business. I would need someone to be there during business hours, to handle sales while I was painting or taking care of other things.

Antonio stopped by sometimes, bringing coffee or asking me to lunch. He never asked me to dinner, tried to come to my apartment, or invited me to his. He took things slow like I wanted, not even touching me.

Without the pressure of romance, it was easier for me to get to know him, to feel comfortable around him when we sat across from each other at lunch or coffee. He always stared at me with a possessive look, like he couldn't wait until I was finally ready for something more.

He hadn't tried to hold me again. Last time, it was so intimate and close that it was too much for both of us. It was too much for me because I wasn't ready for someone new, and it was too much for him because he could hardly restrain himself and keep his promise.

When three months had come and gone, I felt better about the breakup with Bones. I still loved him, would never forget him, but now my chest didn't hurt all the time. My dreams weren't always about him. Throughout the day, he wasn't the only thing on my mind.

It'd been a cruel three months, one of the most difficult periods in my life. I didn't consider myself to be over him, not yet. But I was definitely better now than I was before. I wasn't ready to be with Antonio romantically, but I'd started to let him into my heart.

I was about to close the gallery for the day when Antonio walked inside, a large bag gripped in his hand. "Hope you're hungry. I brought dinner."

"Ooh…I'm always hungry." I'd just finished hanging up a new painting, so I wiped my hands on my jeans then turned to him. "What did you get?"

"I made salmon, rice, and broccoli."

"You made it?" I asked in surprise. "You cook?"

He grinned. "Yep. And I'm pretty good at it." He pulled out the plastic containers and set everything on the floor. The only surface I had was my desk with my computer, but I only had one chair. So eating in the center of the room was our only choice.

"Wow. I'm impressed."

"I'm a man of many talents." He pulled out a bottle of wine and poured two glasses, and he produced two plastic forks.

I sat across from him, the art lights still hitting the paintings. It was bright inside the room compared to the darkness outside. The sun had set, and the buildings blocked any extra light that could have hit the street.

I picked up my fork and dug in. "Wow…this is good."

"Told ya." He scooped the food into his mouth, his chiseled jaw working as he chewed. He washed it down with the white wine and then lifted his gaze to me. "I'm glad you like it."

"Like it? I love it. I've never been able to cook anything. I'm so bad at it."

"I can always teach you."

"I doubt it," I said with a chuckle. "Griffin always…" I stopped myself from talking, knowing it was rude to talk about my ex when Antonio went to all this trouble to make me dinner. I had to be better at that, to not talk about the love of my life every time he popped into my head.

Antonio kept eating like Griffin hadn't been mentioned at all.

"You know about my love life. Can I ask you about yours?"

"What do you want to know?" He finished eating then set his empty container on the hardwood floor.

"I don't know. Have you ever loved someone the way I love Griffin?" Was that too personal of a question? He didn't have to answer anything he didn't feel comfortable with.

"No." He said it quickly, without even having to think about his answer. "Not in the intense way you've described. I've had somewhat serious relationships throughout my twenties. Some that lasted a year or so. But they eventually ran their course and we both moved on."

He didn't describe his romantic life in the way I described mine—at all. It didn't seem like he'd ever really been in love either. He just had one relationship and then the next. "Did you ever love these women?"

"I said that I did," he said. "But now, I realize there are different kinds of love, different levels. I've never felt this all-consuming passion that you describe for Griffin. I've never felt weak in the knees, or like I couldn't live without this person. I was seeing a woman when you and I met. It'd been a few months, but I wouldn't consider it to be serious. But when I met you, I knew something was going to happen. So I ended things with her."

I froze on the spot, unable to believe what I'd just heard. "You left her?"

"I had to." He drank his wine as he looked at me. "I didn't want to keep seeing her while another woman was on my mind. The second I felt our connection, I knew my relationship with her was over anyway. I wanted to pursue this regardless of where it went, and if I stayed with her, it wouldn't fair. She deserves to be with a man who worships her. I realized I wasn't that man…and I made the right decision for both of us."

Speechless, I set my container on the floor, no longer hungry. "I don't know what to say."

"There's nothing to say. I've enjoyed spending time with you even if it's never been romantic. I've gotten a lot more enjoyment out of it than I ever did with her… not to insult her in any way. There's something special here, something everlasting. Something tells me this is where I'm meant to be…when you're ready to have me."

I lowered my gaze, unable to look him in the eye. It was the most romantic thing anyone had ever said to me. "Thank you for being so patient with me. I know it must be frustrating…"

"Not in the least," he said. "And that's how I know you're worth waiting for." He gave me a slight smile before he drank his wine. "Your family is nice. Will they be back sometime soon?"

I was relieved he'd changed the subject, especially when things became too intense. "My brother and sister-in-law are still looking for a place in Tuscany. Sapphire wants to be close to my parents, but Conway doesn't want to be too close."

He chuckled. "Understandable."

"I see Carmen pretty often since our shops are only a few blocks apart."

"What does she do?"

"She runs a flower shop."

"That's wonderful," he said. "So all the Barsettis are extremely successful."

"I don't know about extremely…but we're hard-working people."

He drank his wine again. "Same thing. What are your parents like?"

"Well…my father is the most intense and brooding man you've ever meet. My mother is a breath of fresh air during a sandstorm."

He chuckled. "Good description."

"My father was actually in the gallery when you first asked me out."

"He was?" Antonio was about to finish off his wine, but he steadied his glass instead. "I didn't notice him."

"He was on the other side of this wall." I pointed to the small divider that held two other paintings and separated the gallery into different sections. "He came by to take me to lunch, and I was finishing up some work when you walked in. He heard everything…told everyone in my family about it."

"That must have been awkward," he said with a chuckle. "If I'd known, I definitely would have picked a better time. Sorry about that. I'm not sorry I did that, but I'm sorry that it must have made you uncomfortable."

"No, don't apologize. It's actually the reason why my father likes you. He said he liked your confidence as well as your respect. When I said no, you didn't rush me. But you also had the self-assuredness to take control of the situation. My father is very, very picky when it comes to the men who express interest in me. So there's something about you that he liked."

"Good to know. I'm really glad I stormed in here and demanded a date from you."

I smiled, enjoying his joke. "Me too."

His playful expression faded away when he saw me

smile. His eyes softened noticeably, his affection brightening at the same time. It was the first time I'd acknowledged something romantic about us, had opened up to him in some way, and he definitely noticed. "Can I demand a date from you tomorrow night? Our first date?"

It'd been three months, and there was no going back at this point. Bones and I were done, and I would probably never see him again. The twinge in my heart would fade in time, and maybe I needed to start dating for that discomfort to finally go away. Antonio had been patient with me, and my entire family already liked him. But most importantly, I liked him. "Yeah…I'd love to."

ANTONIO STOOD in front of my painting, his hands resting in his pockets. He took his time in front of each one, examining the colors under the art lights. We left our dinner in the middle of the room, the wine bottle nearly empty because we both had a love of wine. "I really like this one."

I stood beside him, my shoulder almost touching his body. "You said that about the other one."

"Because I mean it." He moved to the left and

examined another painting, an image of a vase with yellow flowers. It was sitting on the counter of Carmen's shop, and the background was full of tools, windows, and other flowers that were ready to be sold. The focal point was the vase, but the real subject was the flower shop in Florence. "Now…I really like this one. The vase is so simple and calm, but everything around it hints at the chaos of running a shop. From the disarrayed tools to the loose petals that have fallen on the tabletop, to Carmen working in the background. So much detail." He continued to stare at it, his arms resting by his sides. Other people loved my paintings too, but he stared at them with professional scrutiny. His eyes were like sponges, soaking up every line and every color. He got lost in my paintings the way I did when I created them. There was no one else in the world who understood my artwork the way he did.

Examining each other's artwork was my favorite pastime. I loved to look at his creations and describe what I felt, and I loved listening to him do the same for my work. We praised one another, dissected one another. I never felt self-conscious about my talent when he examined my pieces. If anything, I felt more confident.

Without looking at me, he moved his hand to mine.

His fingers interlocked between my digits, and he gave me a tight squeeze with his large hand.

My breathing stopped when I felt his touch. Despite how innocent it was, I felt like we were connected in every way possible. I felt the heat between us, the unde-niable chemistry that flowed through our veins. He made me feel alive, banished the shadow that hung over my head. He made me feel invigorated, charged. My breathing started to escalate because the searing connection between us was burning my skin. All we did was hold hands, but it seemed like more than that.

He turned his head my way slightly so he could look at me. "You feel that?"

I nodded.

"When I touch you, I feel what I feel when I look at your paintings. I feel so much…with so little. I've waited a month just to hold your hand, but I'd wait a lifetime for this kind of embrace." He didn't lean in to kiss me or give me a sign that he would try, but holding my hand was intimate enough. He turned to the painting again, getting lost in the colors.

I looked forward again and then rested my head on his shoulder, feeling my heart race even faster as more of our skin touched. It felt wrong, but it also felt right. It would never feel the way it did with Bones, but I certainly felt something.

Antonio turned his head my way and placed a kiss at my hairline, his soft lips touching my warm skin.

I closed my eyes, remembering the last time Bones did the same thing. I missed his kisses, missed the way he used to look at me like I was all that mattered. I still missed him, still loved him. Moving on from him was the hardest thing I'd ever had to do, but I was finally making progress. I couldn't feel guilty for finding someone else, not when I waited three months and gave my heart plenty of time to heal. But even if I did fall in love with Antonio, I knew I would never stop loving Bones.

Never.

THIRTEEN

Bones

———————

I quit drinking six weeks ago.

I hated every second of it.

Losing booze was just as bad as losing Vanessa.

I poured myself into my work because I had nothing else to do with my time. I used to drink a lot, but now that it was taken away from me, I had nothing else to keep busy. The only reason I got clean in the first place was because I'd lost myself to the darkness. Being sober somewhat pulled me out, punished me for the idiotic crime I'd committed.

I had much better control now.

I was in Milan because I'd just come back from a long job. It was in Ireland, and I had a long hit list. Max was giving me lots of work because it made me feel better. The guys got to take time off work, and I got to keep busy. It worked for all of us.

But I couldn't work all the time.

The quiet times when I was alone were the worst. I never thought I would turn into a pussy like this, the kind of man that moped around after he lost a woman. I should have been over Vanessa six weeks after we went our separate ways.

But now it'd been three months—and I still felt like shit.

I hadn't gotten pussy because that never felt right. The few times when the opportunity arose, I changed my mind and went home alone. The only action I got was when my hand was wrapped around my length.

Now I was a pathetic man who jerked off every night.

What the fuck had happened to me?

My original goal was to wipe out the Barsetti line for good. But instead, they destroyed my life—a second time.

I couldn't believe I'd let this happen.

I was sitting in the living room when the elevator beeped to tell me someone was approaching. It had to be Max because he was now the only other one with the code to the building. I'd been sitting on the couch, shirtless, and watching TV. A glass of water sat on the table in front of me.

Fucking piss.

I missed the dark amber liquid of booze. I missed the burn down my throat. I missed the constant buzz my brain was under. Now that I was constantly sober, my mind was clear, and I couldn't keep Vanessa out of my thoughts.

I hated being sober.

It wasn't me.

The only reason I kept my word was because I owed that much to my boys. They were worried about me after that stupid night, and I had to prove to them that the worst had passed. I was in control once more. But I still didn't drink because my name hadn't been cleared yet.

The doors opened, and Max walked inside. "I just wired the cash."

"I saw that."

"You did a great job. No one suspected a thing."

"No one ever suspects a thing."

He glanced at my water glass and then took a look around the apartment. "Are you really going to sell this place?"

As much as I loved this apartment, I couldn't live

here anymore. Vanessa's ghost still drifted in the hallway during the night. Her presence was still in the sheets, on the couch. Sometimes I would find random souvenirs that she'd left behind, like a hair tie in the bathroom drawer or a thong that got stuck to my clothes in the dryer. I kept waiting for it to get easier, but it never did. I needed to start over.

In the back of my mind, I kept waiting for Vanessa to call me and tell me her father changed his mind. I hoped she would have convinced him somehow, had done something to prove to him that what we had was real.

But she didn't succeed.

Now that three months had come and gone, I knew it was really over.

She wasn't coming back.

I had to move on.

"Bones."

I turned to him, my eyes narrowing on his face. "Hmm?"

"You still putting this place up for sale?"

"Yeah," I finally answered. "I'll head up to Lake Garda."

"And where's all this furniture gonna go?"

"I guess I'll take it to the new place, whenever I find one."

He moved to the seat beside me, his arms resting on his knees. He glanced at the water glass again. "I'm surprised you've stuck to it this long."

"Hasn't been easy. I think I've earned the right to go back."

"I don't know about that. You were in a pretty dark place. Having a few drinks might put you there again."

"No. If I really didn't have any control, I wouldn't have been able to stay sober this long. That was a bad mistake, and I'm ready to move on from it."

Max turned his head to look at me, and he watched me with shrewd eyes. "If you were really ready to move on, you would have opened the door to Vanessa's art room by now. But that door has remained shut for three months."

The second she was gone, I shut the door and never opened it again. I pretended it didn't exist, walking past it every single day without even glancing at it. I wanted it to disappear on its own. I should throw all her stuff away, but that seemed like a waste of all her supplies. But I didn't want to hold on to it either, not when I had no use for it. "I don't know what to do with her shit, alright?"

"Yes, you do. You just don't want to do it. That tells me you aren't over it."

"I'll never really be over it, Max." I stared at my

glass of water, which had been untouched since I poured it. Water didn't taste like anything. It was like drinking air. It didn't burn my throat or make me feel good. It was pointless.

"Well, you need to start. You need to be with other women and get back to who you used to be."

"Fucking someone isn't going to magically fix me."

"But it'll start to fix you. You really want to be miserable over this woman forever?"

"No…"

He faced forward again. "We'll toss everything in that room, get you laid, and go back to the way our lives used to be."

The plan sounded so simple, but I still couldn't execute it. Something was holding me back, some misguided hope in my chest. Even though I'd had plenty of time and plenty of closure, I felt like there was something missing. I needed more. "I guess I expected Vanessa to change her father's mind."

"That guy will never change his mind, man. He's stubborn as hell."

"I guess I've always held on to a small bit of hope that something would happen—"

"It's not, Bones. You need to move on."

It'd been three months but I still wasn't ready. I

wasn't prepared to take the plunge, to really say goodbye forever. "I need more…"

"More what?"

"Closure."

"How?" he asked. "What does that mean?"

"I want to see her. Just one more time. I want to see if she's happy, see what her life is like. Maybe she's moved on, and seeing her moved on will help me move on."

"Bullshit, man. You want to see if she's as miserable as you are."

Was there anything wrong with that?

"Nothing good can come from this. Let it go."

"Look—"

"No. You made it this long. Forget about her and move on. It would be more beneficial for you to hook up with a woman in a bar instead of hunting down your ex and stalking her like a weirdo. Frankly, it's pathetic."

I bowed my head, knowing he was right. "I hate being like this. I don't regret loving her, but I regret loving her so much. I regret getting this deep with her. If we'd never told her parents and kept our relationship a secret, I could have enjoyed her longer."

He patted my back. "Don't dwell on it. Just move

on. You could have any woman you want. So go out and get her."

The only woman I wanted was the one I couldn't have.

"You've worked this hard to get here. So don't blow it doing something stupid."

I always did stupid things. The stupidest thing I'd ever done was fall in love with a Barsetti.

And I was even stupider for telling her.

———

THE NEXT DAY, I made the five-hour drive to Florence.

I kept telling myself to turn around and forget this stupid idea. But every time I actually considered turning back, my hand tightened on the wheel and my foot pressed against the gas. I wouldn't find anything good in Florence, nothing that would make me feel better about the relationship, but it might bring me closure.

I wanted to know how she was, how her gallery was doing. I didn't keep tabs on her when I left, knowing watching her would only haunt me. She had the protection of the Barsetti family, so she didn't need me anyway.

I'd been thinking about her every single day since we'd been apart, and I needed to know what her life was like now. Did she stay in the apartment above the gallery? Did she keep the gallery? Had she sold the car? Would I see her in the window of her shop, talking with a customer who'd just bought a painting? Would she wear a fake smile, hiding her inner turmoil? Or would her smile be real?

Was she over me?

Hours later, I arrived in the city. The sun was starting to go down, and couples walked on the sidewalks as they headed to dinner. I navigated through the motorcyclists and turned on a few narrow streets until I arrived on her street.

This was my first stop after I left her at the house. I wrote the note and left it on the table, my parting words to her. I didn't tell her I loved her. It seemed redundant at that point. If I didn't love her, I would have just kidnapped her and took her to some remote place in the world where her family would never find us. Even if she wanted to escape, I wouldn't have allowed it. Instead, I let her go, knowing she needed her family more than she needed me.

But that didn't mean shit to her father.

I hated Pearl Barsetti for ruining my inheritance.

But I hated Crow Barsetti so much more.

He ruined my life.

I could be with Vanessa right at that very moment, having dinner together at the dining table. I might be her husband right now. I might be sharing my life with her. But that piece of shit took that away.

There was a vacant parking spot across the street from her gallery, so I pulled into the space and parked. I was in a white Fiat, blending in with all the other cars on the street. My truck was totaled, so I would never have that again. I wore a black baseball cap, hiding my features as much as possible.

The lights were still on in her gallery. I looked through the window, waiting to see her walk by. My heart pounded in my chest with angst. The pulse in my ears was like ringing bells. I didn't want to see her, but at the same time, I couldn't drive away until I did.

What did I expect to see? What did I expect to accomplish?

She moved into my line of sight, her dark hair done in nice curls. Her olive skin was the same, deep in intensity and soft in appearance. She wore a blue dress, sandals on her feet. My eyes had been so focused on her that I didn't notice the man beside her.

Italian in appearance, over a foot taller than her, etched in obvious muscularity. I could tell he was a young man who was similar in age. He stood directly beside her, their bodies not touching. They were staring at the painting on the wall.

Before I panicked and smashed the window, I reminded myself that she wasn't just an artist, but a businesswoman, so she needed to sell her work for a profit. That's all he was, just a customer.

But even if he wasn't, it shouldn't matter.

I watched them for a few more minutes, saw them move from one painting to the next. She should be closed by now, but maybe she stayed open in the hopes of making a sale. Maybe he wanted to buy several pieces.

She wasn't mine anymore. It shouldn't matter.

Then I saw something that ripped my heart cleanly in two. It hurt more than saying goodbye to her. It hurt more than the tears I'd shed on that cruel afternoon. Like everything I'd believed had come raining down, the air left my lungs.

He grabbed her hand and interlocked their fingers together.

Pain. Unbearable pain.

Betrayal.

Hot rage.

I felt a tumult of emotions, ranging from anger to jealousy to emptiness.

Then she rested her head on his shoulder.

The affection was clear. They examined her paintings together as a couple, not as an owner and a customer. He probably worshiped her work, and he was telling her how talented she was at that very moment. It wasn't clear whether this was a new relationship or one that had been going for a while. The fact that they were alone together in her gallery when it was closed told me he wasn't a stranger.

She knew him well.

Had probably already slept with him.

I wanted to smash the window of my car.

Smash the windows of her gallery.

Strangle him until he choked to death.

The same rush of adrenaline burst through me, the very kind I experienced before I killed someone. I wanted to kill this man, and I was grateful I couldn't see his face so it couldn't haunt me later.

I had to remind myself that this was inevitable. She couldn't be alone forever. Whether she waited a few weeks or a few months, it shouldn't matter. I knew she loved me. I knew what we had was real. If we couldn't be together, she should be happy.

Be happy without me.

Maybe this was the man she wanted, someone her family would adopt into their ranks. Maybe he wasn't a murderer like I was. Maybe he was clean-cut and boring, respecting her like a gentleman and taking her antique shopping.

Maybe he was better than me.

Maybe he was better than I'd ever been.

No, I couldn't be angry with her. I couldn't be jealous either.

This was how it was supposed to be.

I was a bad man, a killer and a criminal. I got off on spilled blood. I got off on putting bullets in my enemies. I was a man of the shadows, of the underworld. I liked booze, women, and bullets. I liked paying for sex so I could get exactly what I wanted. I liked not feeling anything, besides murderous rage.

She was a flower, a flower that belonged in the sun. She needed to be pampered, to sway in the wind under the sky. She was innocent, pure, and beautiful. She wanted a husband, a father for her children. She wanted to have dinner with her family every Sunday night underneath the olive trees. She wanted everything that life had to give, all the beauty, hope, and serenity.

I wasn't right for her.

I wasn't good enough for her.

We were from different worlds.

And we should stay in different worlds.

I turned the engine back on, and without looking at

her again, I pulled onto the road and drove away. I gripped the steering wheel and refused to glance in the rearview mirror to see if they were walking out of the gallery and to her apartment. I focused my gaze straight ahead, leaving the past behind me for good. "Goodbye, Vanessa."

FOURTEEN

Carter

I looked at the schematic of the new model I'd created. The design of the exterior was just as important as all the gadgets under the hood and inside the vehicle. From the special formation of the leather seats, to the impressive technology with the touch screen, people wanted the kind of car that both impressed and pissed off others at the same time.

I was sitting at my desk in my office, in my home situated just outside of Milan. I was in between the city and Verona, having a few acres to myself and a home surrounded by fortifications to keep the people I didn't want to see off my property.

I lived under the radar, not because I had anything to hide; I just didn't like people.

Anyone, really.

I like cars, sex, and booze. That was my well-rounded life.

And I liked it.

Conway had settled down and taken a wife. With a baby on the way, he'd turned into a family man. I'd seen him fuck three women at once. I'd seen him live in the shadows as well as I did, belonging there without question. But now he'd completely flipped, washing his hands of his past and taking on a new identity.

At least he was happy.

A domesticated life like that would never make me happy. I lived my life just the way I was behind the wheel, always going at full speed. Instead of slowing down and avoiding my obstacles, I liked to swerve out of the way and hope for the best.

I'd never take a wife.

Shit, I wouldn't even take a girlfriend.

My parents never gave me shit about it. Carmen was a beautiful woman, and she would definitely give them grandkids. She was my saving grace, taking that kind of attention from my parents so they would ignore me.

I didn't think Conway made a mistake. Sapphire was exquisite, and since she had a special quality that obsessed him, she seemed to be a good match. And she didn't seem to care about his billions either.

But I still couldn't believe it happened.

I was a bigger asshole than my cousin, rough around the edges in a way he never was. I didn't think before I spoke, and as a result, I pissed off a lot of people. But that was fine with me. I preferred to be transparent, so people would know exactly what they were getting from me. They didn't have unrealistic expectations.

Carter Barsetti was cold, ruthless, and a bit of an asshole.

My phone rang on the desk, and I paused with my schematic to check the number. It was a number I didn't recognize, from a country code somewhere near Russia. Just because I didn't recognize a number didn't mean it wasn't important. I took the call. "Carter." I kept looking at my drawing of the new model, only giving half my attention to the phone call.

"Egor Sokolov. Nice to meet you, Carter Barsetti." A heavy Russian accent came over the line, naturally formidable.

That name didn't mean anything to me. "What can I do for you?"

"I'm glad you asked. My younger sister was taken by the Skull Kings. I've been told you're the only person who can recover women in this circumstance." For a man who'd lost his sister, he didn't seem choked up about it. He spoke with a pragmatic tone, like we were discussing what kind of paint job a car should have. Most of my clients were either panicked or somewhat emotional. I'd heard grown men cry over the phone as they begged me to save their daughter.

"I used to be in that business. I'm not anymore."

Heavy silence fell, the kind that was full of explosive disappointment. "I'm sure you can make an exception."

I made a promise to my father, and I was the kind of man that kept promises. "I've been out of the game for a while. Too much liability. I'm sorry about your sister but—"

"Name your price."

I'd never heard a man make that kind of offer. "I'm really not—"

"Any price."

I sat back in my leather chair, my eyes narrowing on nothing in particular. I squeezed the pen in my hand, my nostrils flaring with hostility. "Interrupt me one more time, and see what happens. I'll fly over there to the wasteland you live in and shove a pistol up your ass and pull the trigger." No one came to me and asked for a favor then turned around and interrupted me. That shit wasn't going to fly.

Egor turned quiet, his annoyance simmering. After

a while, he spoke. "My apologies." His voice was restrained, like he was forcing himself to say the words even though it was the last thing he wanted to do. "My sister is very important to me, Carter. I understand you aren't in the business anymore, but perhaps this could be your last job. I'm willing to pay you anything to make it happen."

The highest amount I'd ever been paid was fifty million dollars, and that was a fluke. But that wasn't enough to get me to change my mind. "I'm sorry, Egor. But it's not going to happen. The Skull Kings are the kind of psychopaths you don't want to cross."

"You've been crossing them for years."

"Yes. And I got out before it became a problem."

"Then one more time won't hurt."

I chuckled. "Persistent, huh?"

"Carter, how does a hundred million sound?"

That was double the highest amount I'd been paid. Most people offered between ten and fifteen million. This was definitely the most lucrative offer I'd ever received. It was enough to get my attention.

"We have a deal?"

The money was enticing, especially since the payday was so easy. All I had to do was bid on her then hand her over. It was a simple transaction. But then my father's words haunted me. I was close with my father, and I didn't want to disappoint him. "I made a promise to someone that I would stay out of the game."

"It's only one time. No one will know."

He was probably right, but was it worth the risk?

"One-fifty."

A hundred and fifty million? "Your sister must be one hell of a woman."

His smile was audible. "Yes. She is."

Now, I was seriously tempted. I would get in, get out, and never show my face again. I wasn't Conway Barsetti, but everyone in our circles knew how close we were. The Skull Kings would allow me inside, especially if I told them I was working on my cousin's behalf. I could do it one time, and no one would ever know.

It would be the easiest fortune I'd ever made.

Egor's voice burned through the phone. "So, you in?"

I still didn't give my answer.

"Come on, Carter. It's the easiest one-fifty you've ever made."

I should turn him down and move on with my life. It wasn't like I was pressed for cash. I had more money than I needed. Having more wouldn't change my life that much. But turning down that much cash for only a day of work sounded stupid.

Even my father would understand that.

"Alright," I said. "I'm in."

"Good," he said. "I knew you would come around. Before we finalize anything, there's something else I need you to do."

"I'm listening."

"I need you to hold on to my sister for a while before you give her back to me."

"That's fine. That's how it has to be anyway." If I gave her back too soon, the Skull Kings would be on to me.

"Good. I'll be in Saudi Arabia for business for a while. And I don't trust my men with her."

His men? Why would his sister be with his men?

"And I'm sure I don't need to warn you to stay away from my sister, right?" The threat was obvious.

I never slept with the women I rescued from the Underground. "Rape isn't my style, not when I already have more pussy than I can handle."

"Just the answer I wanted to hear. As a thank you, I'll wire the fee to your account up front."

That would make babysitting his sister a lot more bearable. I wasn't looking forward to sharing my space with some woman, to sacrificing my privacy. I would have to talk to her, make sure she had what she needed, and keep her hidden from the public eye. "Very kind of you."

"Let me know when you have her."

"Sure thing."

He didn't say goodbye before hanging up.

I tossed the phone on the surface and pondered the decision I'd just made. It was risky and stupid, but when I thought of the pile of money being dropped into my bank account at that very moment, I didn't care about my stupidity.

It would go the way it always went, smooth and simple. The most difficult part would be keeping the woman entertained in my home. After everything she'd been through with the Skull Kings, she would probably be timid and quiet. She would want nothing to do with me, too afraid that I might do something to her too. Most of the time, Conway took the girls and circulated them through his model roster so I didn't have to deal with this shit, but I could handle it one more time.

How hard could it be?

I GOT into the Underground without trouble, stepping in as Conway's replacement. They all knew me there, recognized my face easily enough, and while they raised their eyebrows before they let me in, they didn't ask any questions.

I took my seat, ordered a drink, and waited.

I was alone at my table, as were the other men in the room. Each sat at a dark table with a lone candle, sipping their drinks as they waited for the auctions to begin. Most men didn't socialize even if they knew each other. They wanted to pretend that the evening wasn't happening, that they weren't there at all.

It was Italy's most open secret.

The auction finally began, and the girls were forced onto the stage, buck naked and handcuffed. Heels were on their feet, but that was the only item of clothing they were given. Black stilettos, the shoes were tall with a pointed toe.

There were six of them that evening, some more beautiful than others. But their allure wasn't always in their beauty, but instead their connection to whichever family had been targeted. A man could still get off with an ugly woman if she was the daughter of a prince he disliked. Sometimes sex wasn't about physical attraction, but power.

But there was one woman in particular who exuded pure beauty. With dark strands of hair that framed her face, full lips outlined in bright red lipstick, and lightly colored brown eyes, she was stunning. A few freckles sprinkled across her cheeks, but that added to her allure. She was of average height, probably a head shorter than me. While the other women could barely make eye contact because they were shaking so much, she seemed to be the only one unafraid. She looked into the sea of faces in the crowd like she was fearless.

It was just an act, but I still respected her for it.

These men like terrified women. They liked women who trembled in the presence of power. They liked helpless girls who begged for freedom they would never get. But this woman wasn't like the others.

The other men noticed her too, judging by the way they watched her closely and ignored the others.

The bid would probably run high.

Egor had texted me a picture of his sister, an image I'd barely glanced at last night. I pulled my phone from my pocket and checked the screen to confirm her identity. The woman was sitting under an apple tree on a sunny day. She was smiling at the camera, her hair blowing in the wind.

It was the beautiful one.

I slipped my phone back into my pocket and refused to celebrate my excitement. It didn't matter if I was hard in my jeans from seeing that naked woman on the stage. When I took her home, I couldn't enjoy her.

She was nothing but inventory. This was a job—a job I'd already been paid for.

My eyes moved up her body, taking in her lean legs all the way to her hips. She had an hourglass shape, a sexy waist with even sexier tits. I'd been with seductive women before, but she definitely stood out from the rest. With slender shoulders and beautiful skin, she was absolutely luscious.

I could practically hear all the men drooling.

Her eyes scanned the room, searching the sea of faces like she was looking for something in particular. It didn't make any sense for her to be so fearless when all the other girls were terrified. Some were even crying, sobbing their hearts out.

But she wasn't afraid at all.

It was like she wanted to be there.

I dismissed the thought because that couldn't be possible. She was taken from her home, taken from her family to be a sex slave. In her bleak mind, she had no idea her brother had paid a fortune to save her. The remainder of her life would be spent in horrifying ways.

THE AUCTION WAS INTENSE.

All the men wanted her.

Even if I had to spend a fortune to buy her, I would still be left with an immense profit. So I kept sticking my paddle in the air, battling the other demons in the underworld for her. She was the first woman on the roster, probably because the Skull Kings knew the men wouldn't care about the rest of the girls until their best girl was out of the running.

We were already at thirty million and going strong.

Losing wasn't an option, so I kept bidding on her, making the price skyrocket higher and higher.

The woman stood tall on the stage, her beautiful tits perky and round. Her eyes were on me, watching me bid on her like an antique painting at an art show. Again, there wasn't fear in the look.

Back and forth we went, and eventually, I won the auction.

"And Carter Barsetti wins at fifty million." The Skull King clanked the mallet against the podium. "Enjoy your prize."

Her handcuffs were removed from her wrists, and she was directed off the stage to the floor. She glanced at her arms and massaged her wrists, soothing the marks and scars along her skin where the metal had been too tight. She slowly made her way to me, her head held high even though she was still naked, stripped of the privilege of clothes.

I watched her move toward me, my eyes taking in her curves and her looks. She wasn't given anything to wear, not even a thong, so I could clearly see the small amount of hair between her legs, along with her nub.

I shouldn't look when I couldn't touch, but I didn't have a lot of self-control. I pulled out the chair beside me and snapped my fingers.

Her eyes widened noticeably, offended that I'd addressed her like a dog instead of a person.

I had to exude power and dominance when I was around my fellow demons, so I snapped my fingers again, this time giving her a terrifying look that she would be stupid to defy. "Sit. Now."

She hesitated before she sat down, her bare ass hitting the cushion of the chair. She immediately crossed her legs, hiding her intimate place from view, and then she adjusted her hair in front of her shoulders, making the strands conceal her nipples.

Maybe she was a little afraid.

The auction continued, and I bid on another girl. I couldn't just show my interest in one woman and leave. That would be too obvious. So I raised my paddle into the air, pretending I was seriously interested in one woman when I had no intention of taking her home.

My slave looked at me, her arms crossed over her chest so she could hide her tits from me. She gave me a special look, a look of disgust. "You really need two women?"

I raised my paddle and looked at her at the same time, floored that she cared enough to even ask. Every slave I'd dealt with stayed utterly silent and never asked any questions. They did their best to disappear from my sight, to go unnoticed. This woman didn't seem to care. "I thought you could use the company."

"Because you can't keep me company enough?" Her deep and sensual voice trailed all the way down my spine, digging into the muscles of my back. As if she'd sprinkled a spell over my mind, I forgot about my current situation and failed to raise my paddle to continue the bid. I didn't want the girl anyway, so it didn't matter, but I didn't appreciate the fact that I'd allowed some woman to distract me.

"I'm not the kind of company you want, sweetheart."

"Don't call me sweetheart."

"How about slave?" I snapped. "Do you prefer that?"

Her eyes shifted back and forth as she looked into mine, clearly appalled by the term.

"Sweetheart, it is." I raised my paddle again and started the next bid.

She finally turned away, her attitude still palpable even though I'd subdued the argument. Her fierce brown eyes surveyed the room around her, as if she were searching for all the possible escape routes.

She wouldn't find any.

I PLAYED my part and walked out with the woman I'd paid for. I was in a full suit and tie, so I pulled off my jacket and draped it around her shoulders, hiding her nakedness so she wouldn't have to try to cover herself with her slender arms and long hair.

The second she felt the material against her skin, she yanked it tighter around her body, wrapping herself up so all of her important features were hidden away. The bottom of my jacket hit her knees, so even her ass was covered. She held tight to the material with clenched fingers, clinging to it like a life raft in the middle of the frigid ocean.

The other girls weren't so lucky. Their handcuffs were changed for shackles before they were shoved into the backs of limos. They weren't given clothes. In fact, their heels were ripped off and forced to remain behind. And they were greeted with a backhand from their master.

This woman had no idea how lucky she was.

If my sister were ever in the same circumstance, there was no amount of money I wouldn't pay for her. Barsettis were ruthlessly loyal to one another, taking the definition of family to a new level. If that weren't true, Vanessa wouldn't have ended things with Bones. We were loyal to each other—and no one else.

This woman was lucky her brother cared about her so deeply. Or maybe she was just lucky he was so rich, rich enough that he could drop that kind of cash without thinking twice about it.

I opened the car door for her, one of the cars I'd designed. Worth a million euros, it was the most expensive car in the world. It had the kind of engine that provided the car with enough velocity to send it to the moon.

She peered into the dark car, hesitant before taking the final step inside.

"Get. In." I didn't have the patience for this, not when she was out of danger.

She didn't look at me before she got into the car. She never put on her safety belt, but I didn't care if she did or not.

I got behind the wheel and took off, driving through

the dark and quiet streets of Milan. There was no one else on the road because it was three in the morning. The only people out right now were those who operated under the law—or against it.

The cars that were at the Underground quickly scattered, retreating to their hideaways in different sectors of the city. I sped through the streets, ran the red lights, and made it out of the city within minutes.

The woman kept looking at her surroundings, as if she was trying to determine exactly where she was. She glanced at the speedometer a few times, checking our speed. Thankfully, she didn't ask me a million questions.

I wasn't much of a talker. "We're in Milan."

She turned to me, her lustrous hair falling around her shoulders as she turned her head. With big and bright eyes, her features were fundamentally expressive. It was not difficult to see her emotions because they always danced on the surface of her eyes. Her mouth was just as easy to read, from the way she pressed her lips tightly together to the way she chewed on the corner of her mouth. She faced forward again, dismissing what I'd said. "I'm not a cop, but I think you're supposed to stop at the red lights."

Again, she ran her mouth when she had no right to. She was a prisoner of the Skull Kings, and now she was a prisoner again—to me. Was she stupid? Talking back to me was the quickest way for her to get killed. "I just bought a woman like a piece of livestock. You think I give a shit about the law?" I kept my eyes on her and slammed my foot against the pedal, making the engine roar as the car picked up speed.

She didn't look at me, her eyes glued out the passenger window. We'd just left the city, and now we were on a small road toward the countryside. Vineyards and farms were the only things separating Milan and Verona. My home was somewhere in between. "You just bought me for fifty million euros. You don't need to impress me with the speed of your car."

I laughed because it was ridiculous. "I don't give a damn about impressing you, sweetheart."

"Well, if you don't want me to throw up in your fancy car, I suggest you slow down. I get car sick."

"You just stood buck naked on a stage as you were sold off, vomit-free. But a fast car is your breaking point?"

"Fine." She crossed her arms over her chest as she kicked off her heels. "I'll just throw up in your car, then. Makes no difference to me."

I could buy another car at the drop of a hat, but this was the first vehicle assembled of the new model. I always kept the first ones manufactured, collecting them like trophies. So this car did have some significance to me. I didn't want her vomit to destroy the Italian leather. And I didn't want it to smell like barf forever.

I took my foot off the gas.

The car finally slowed down, reaching the speed limit.

She kept her gaze out the window.

"You're welcome."

"No, you're welcome," she hissed. "Now your precious car won't be ruined."

I kept one hand on the wheel and glanced at her, shocked that this woman was so brazen in her stupidity. Even if I really was some sick pervert who wanted to buy her for my own amusement, she was playing a risky game. She reminded me of Vanessa in that regard— but that wasn't a compliment. "You want to die tonight, sweetheart? Because you're acting like you have a death wish." I glanced at the road again, seeing two headlights coming toward me.

She faced forward, her eyes reflecting the brightness from the approaching car.

"Cut the attitude. You might live a little longer."

She finally shut her mouth, sitting in silence instead of releasing a smartass comment.

"Good. That's better—"

Just as the oncoming car passed, she opened the passenger door and rolled out.

She jumped out of my fucking car.

In nothing but a jacket.

It took me three seconds to process what had happened, to slam my foot on the brakes and force my beloved tires to scrape against the pavement. Smoke rose into the air and my nose as the rubber burned, and my eyes started to smart with the smell and the rage.

That woman just ditched my car.

Jesus Christ.

I flung my seat belt off and pressed my thumb into the panel on the dashboard, making the center console unlock after it read my thumbprint. I pulled out the fully loaded pistol and jumped out of the car. "Get your ass back here."

It was pitch black because we were away from the city. There weren't even any streetlights along this road. The car that had just passed had bright red taillights. The driver probably didn't notice the woman throw herself from my car since it was dark and we were speeding past each other in different directions.

She'd timed her departure to catch the attention of the car, but she didn't time it properly and missed her chance by a few seconds. Now she was out in the middle of nowhere.

I'd never chased down a fugitive like this, but it couldn't be that hard. She couldn't be that fast, not barefoot. She wouldn't risk coming toward me, so she would head for Milan back the way she came.

I started to jog, my feet hitting the pavement as I scanned the grass beside the road. It was slightly untamed so it could hide her body somewhat, but it was too short to hide her completely. The fact that I couldn't see her running told me she was crouched down, hoping I wouldn't be able to spot her in the darkness.

I pulled the small flashlight from my pocket and clicked the button, illuminating the field in front of me.

There she was.

I aimed my gun. "Don't you fucking—"

She took off at a dead sprint, moving at the speed of a bullet.

Shit, she was fast.

I pointed the gun past her shoulder and pulled the trigger, the sound of the gun echoing across the dark pastures. It was loud, so loud that it made her fumble to the ground.

I sprinted hard, catching up to her within a few seconds.

She got to her feet and started to run again, picking up speed remarkably fast.

But I was faster.

I grabbed her by the neck and put her in a choke hold, jerking her off the road and into the grass so I could force her to the ground.

She kicked her legs and threw her arms back, doing everything she possibly could to hit me. She was overwhelmed, but that didn't stop her from fighting. She pushed against me with all her strength, refusing to give up even when the fight was lost.

I squeezed her neck tighter, having no choice but to knock her out. "You'll pay for this later, sweetheart." I cut off the air supply to her lungs and pressed her hard into the ground, overcoming her small frame with my size and strength. The jacket was coming loose and revealing her nakedness, but now I had no respect for her vanity. I'd underestimated this woman, and as a result, she caught me off guard.

I wouldn't make the same mistake twice.

Her movements lessened as her brain slipped away from the lack of oxygen. Finally, she went still, her body limp in my arms.

I held her for a few more seconds, just to make sure this wasn't another trick. Then I let her go, looking down at her in the grass. I shone my flashlight on her, staring at her slightly parted lips and the way her chest rose and fell with her breathing.

I wasn't sure whether I admired this woman or despised her.

I should have told her I was saving her the second we got into the car. But judging by how paranoid she was, she probably wouldn't have believed me anyway.

I gathered her into my arms and carried her back to the car, which was still on. I got her in the passenger seat before I sat down behind the wheel, keeping my gun in my hand this time. I pulled onto the road, grateful no one had witnessed the action that had just taken place.

When I glanced at her in the passenger seat, she was still dead asleep. Her head rested against the window, and she seemed harmless when she was unconscious. She was definitely a lot prettier when her mouth was shut.

I reflected back on my conversation with this mystery woman, this woman without a name. Every smartass comment that flew out of her mouth was in an American accent. It wasn't Russian, like her brother Egor. There could be an explanation for that, but I found it strange all the same.

Something told me I was missing something here.

And I intended to figure it out.

I SHACKLED her ankles and secured her to the frame of the bed. I left her hands free because there was nothing she could do without her legs. I'd give her the dignity to scratch her nose if it itched, even if she didn't deserve it.

Just to be safe, I inserted a tracker into her ankle. That way, I could see exactly where she was if she managed to slip through my fingers again. The area started to bleed slightly, so I placed a small bandage over the site. This woman obviously wasn't trained in self-defense, but she still had the grit to fight me. She thought I was a psychopath who would rape her and kill her, so of course, she fought as hard as she could. I would have told her I was actually her savior, but she was too busy running that mouth of hers.

I left her on the bed, my large jacket still covering her body. I threw an extra blanket over her, just to make her feel more comfortable. I left her there then went to my bedroom down the hallway. My hands were covered in dirt from forcing her to the ground, and there was a scratch on my watch from scraping it against a rock. I rinsed my hands, took a shower, and then called Egor.

"How'd it go?" he asked the second he picked up the phone.

Shitty. That's how it went. "She's asleep down the hall."

"And it went smoothly?"

No, just shitty. "She didn't go quietly, if that's what you mean. I've got her ankles shackled to the bed frame since she's a flight risk. When I drove her home, she jumped out of the car...out of a moving car." I shook my head. "She's crazy."

He chuckled into the phone. "She keeps you on your toes. But that's what I like about her. She's got an ass that won't quit and a mouth that won't shut."

Very strange way to describe your sister. "I would have told her I was rescuing her instead of keeping her, but she was insulting me left and right, and before I had a chance, I was chasing her into a field. But I'll tell her when she wakes up."

"About that..."

I stopped in the center of my bedroom, near the foot of my king-size bed. I had a big window that over-looked the countryside, and there was a large flat-screen TV over the fireplace.

"I'd appreciate it if you didn't confide that information to her."

Why the hell not?

"I'll be out of the country for a while and I can't

retrieve her, so I want to teach her a lesson while she's there."

Teach her a lesson? She was just stripped naked in front of a group of demons and auctioned off like a piece of livestock. She didn't seem afraid, but there was no way she wasn't. I didn't mention that to him, because if I were in his shoes, I wouldn't want to think about my sister being treated that way. "I don't follow, Egor."

"It was her stupidity that got her captured in the first place. I tried to protect her. I tried to get her to listen to me, but she was too damn stubborn. Now look where she's at. She's lucky I had the power to get her out of that situation. If she knows she's safe, there won't be a lesson to learn. So keep her in the dark, Carter."

"That wasn't part of the deal."

"I just paid you a fortune. It can be part of the deal if I want it to be." He turned hostile quickly, his seething anger spilling over the line.

"How am I supposed to deal with her?"

"In whatever way you feel is necessary. Put her in a room, chain her to the wall, and threaten to kill her if she tries to leave. Pretty simple."

I paced across the hardwood floor, my bare feet hitting the rug around my bed. "You want me to threaten your sister?" Now this wasn't making any sense. How could he give me authorization to treat her that way?

"Yes."

My right eyebrow slowly rose toward the ceiling.

"Do whatever you need to do to control her. We'll make the exchange a month from now, and I know she'll be so happy to see me. Do we have an understanding, Carter?"

He wanted me to pretend to be something I wasn't, a slave owner. He wanted me to take this woman's rights away, to keep her locked up like a prisoner. "It's more complicated than that. What reason do I have to keep her? Why did I buy her if I'm just leaving her in a room for a month?" The only reason men spent a fortune on a beautiful woman was to fuck her. If I wasn't doing that, what other purpose was there?

"Good point," he said. "Then enjoy her, Carter. I think you've earned it."

I halted in my tracks, considering what he'd just said with trepidation. This man gave me permission to rape his sister, to do whatever I wanted to her until she was in his possession again. I hadn't reached this level of success by being a stupid man. I was observant and intuitive, and I knew all of this was bullshit. "She's not your sister."

Egor didn't respond, but the silence was full of his amusement.

This man wasn't related to her at all. I didn't know that backstory or how she got stuck with the Skull Kings to begin with, but I knew I'd stepped into another shadow of the underworld. The smart thing to do was not ask any questions. Once I handed the woman over, my hands would no longer be dirty in this twisted narrative. I did this for the money and no other reason. The specifics were none of my concern.

Egor released a malevolent chuckle over the line. "Who I am doesn't matter. Just keep her in line until I'm back. We'll make the trade, and your job will be done, Carter. Easiest fortune you've ever made."

I WAS up early the next morning, drinking coffee at the dining table when I heard my guest's voice. It wasn't sexy and husky like it had been the night before. Now it was explosive, even more combative than it was last night. "Asshole! Get your ass in here and let me go!"

I set the coffee mug down, the cup still steaming because I'd just poured it. I was shirtless and in my sweatpants, my hair still slightly damp from the shower I'd taken. Normally, I would be reading the paper right now, but my thoughts were focused on the handful I had upstairs. She would be my prisoner for a month until Egor came to collect her.

What the hell was I supposed to do with her?

She wasn't quiet and timid like the others, which meant she would interfere with my personal life. How would I get laid if it seemed like I had a prisoner in the house? If she kept being this argumentative, I would have to move her down to the basement so no one would hear her.

Or I'd have to threaten her.

She had no idea who I was or what I was capable of, so if I gave her a serious scare, she might be more cooperative.

Shouldn't be difficult for me to do.

"Hey, Bitch-hole!"

My eyebrows almost jumped off my face. "Bitch-hole?" I said to myself.

"Get up here now!"

She was in no position to make demands, but she did it anyway. It was amusing and impressive. I finally left my coffee behind and made my way upstairs to her bedroom. Her legs were up on the bed, but her upper body had tipped over the mattress so her torso was on the floor. The jacket had come loose, so one of her tits was popping out. She looked unbelievably uncomfortable, and it was clear she'd been trying to find a way to get out of the chains.

When I looked at the foot of the bed, I saw the wood had been chipped by her chains. She's been yanking on it for hours, doing her best to break free, but then she pulled too hard and toppled over—getting stuck in this compromising position.

I leaned against the doorframe, my arms across my chest. I cocked my head as I stared at her, not being a gentleman any longer. I stared at her openly, looking at her tit without guilt. Her left boob was firm and round, and her nipple hardened under my stare. "Bitch-hole?"

She yanked the jacket over her body, covering her tits from view. "It's bitch and asshole mixed together…"

She really did have a nice rack. She had a nice everything. "Since I'm a bitch-hole, maybe I should rip that jacket off?"

She continued to grip the jacket, prepared to fight me for it.

"And then I should put you on your stomach and fuck that sexy little asshole of yours?" The second I made the threat, the bumps erupted down my arms. As a man who got action on a regular basis, I wasn't hard-pressed for sex, but seeing a vulnerable woman like this tempted me.

I liked the chains, the helplessness, and I also liked the fight. I wanted to silence that mouth of hers and fuck her into submission. She was wild, but I wanted to tame her. I wanted to seize the power and make her tremble in fear.

I'd never wanted that before.

But I was better than that. I'd never been that kind of man. I wasn't necessarily a good man, but I wasn't evil either.

Or perhaps I'd misjudged myself.

I examined her with a harder stare, my eyes narrowing. "It's nice when you don't talk."

Like the spitfire that she was, she immediately snapped back. "Fuck off."

"You want me to help you or not?"

"Yes. I want you to take these damn chains off me so I can use the bathroom. Didn't realize that was so much to ask."

"It is." I crossed the floor to the foot of the bed and unlocked the shackles from around her ankles.

The second she was free, she kicked me in the chest, bucking like a wild horse.

I smiled, anticipating the move. I grabbed her right foot and flipped her over instantly, the muscles of my arms and core exceeding her strength a million times over. I forced her onto her stomach, being as ruthless as possible. I might have underestimated her once, but she should never underestimate me.

I pushed her jacket up to reveal her ass, two curved and rounded cheeks, and then settled on top of her. This was just an empty threat, a way to terrify her, but I couldn't help but get hard. I got off on her fight, on the sight of her beautiful body on the bedroom floor. She did her best to escape my hold, and feeling her weakness in comparison to my strength got me harder than a steel rod.

"Get off me!" She fought against me, doing her best to buck me off with her hips.

I was the weight of a horse, so her bucks were pointless. I pushed my sweatpants and boxers down, revealing my long and thick cock before I grabbed both of her wrists and pinned them against the hardwood floor.

Now, I wanted this even more.

I'd never wanted to fuck a woman like this.

The power was like a drug, and I was higher than a kite. I wanted to punish her for mouthing off to me. I wanted to teach her a lesson for fighting against me. I wanted to fuck her against the floor, using her however I wanted. The power was intoxicating.

"Don't."

I wasn't sure what I was doing anymore. This

started off as a stunt, but now that my pants were down and my big cock was pressed in between her soft cheeks, I didn't know if it was just for show anymore. My cock throbbed for her pussy, throbbed for her fight. I wanted to slide into her slit, whether she was wet or not. I wanted to cross a line I'd never crossed before, to take advantage of my station above this woman.

"I said no."

I pressed the tip of my cock against her entrance, feeling her soft flesh with my sensitive head. My mouth moved to her ear, my breaths coming out shaky from desire. Blood was pounding in my veins, mixed with arousal and adrenaline. "I don't give a damn what you said. No means nothing, not in my house. I will fuck you just like this on the floor and stuff your pussy with my come. And I will enjoy every goddamn second of it."

She heaved underneath me, finally dropped her no-bullshit attitude and showed the first signs of fear. She wasn't the brave woman who jumped out of the moving car. Now she was just a woman trying to protect her dignity.

My cock was still hard, ready to slide into that tight slit and dump all my arousal inside her, but the second she abandoned her guarded ferocity and turned into a vulnerable woman, her words finally got through to me.

Her plea for respect resonated with me, and I knew if I went through with it, even if I had every right to and no one would ever know, I wouldn't like myself.

I wouldn't be any different from the men I'd bought her from.

A real man shouldn't have to force a woman for sex. A real man should get offers left and right. That was who I was, Carter Barsetti, one of the most eligible bachelors in Italy, a billionaire with more pussy than he knew what to do with.

But I finally had this woman where I wanted her —afraid.

I pressed my lips against her ear, putting more weight on her small frame. "Don't fuck with me again."

She breathed harder, her body tensing up even more.

"You understand, sweetheart?" My cock was still at her entrance, desperate to sink into that womanly flesh and disappear. I could feel her back rise against my chest when she breathed, feel her frantic pulse thud against my body. Both of her wrists were pounding with fear from her beating heart. I'd finally terrified her enough to make her think before she ran that smartass mouth.

"Yes…"

"I'm a very rich man. Paying fifty million for you

was like buying a hot coffee at a bakery, pennies to me. If you keep being a pain in the ass, I'll kill you like all the others—and buy another replacement."

AFTER I LET her use the bathroom and wash her face, I chained her back up to the bed and left the room.

This time, she didn't complain.

She didn't even look at me.

I had no idea what I was going to do with her at this point. She was finally subdued, but based on her previous behavior, she would probably take another shot at escape. She probably wouldn't refrain from killing me either, if she had the opportunity. I cleared the house of the guns I'd stored in random places, knowing she would search if she ever got the chance.

But I couldn't keep her tied up like that forever. If I did, I'd have to babysit her night and day. I'd have to hire a crew to keep an eye on her when I left the house. And if I brought women back home, I'd have to make sure she didn't make a peep. I couldn't let my guests think I was a kidnapper, not with my somewhat famous profile.

So what was I going to do with her?

Tough question.

Making her my personal slave was tempting. Chaining her to my headboard and fucking her all I wanted made me hard just thinking about it. A strong woman was sexy, but a defiant one was even sexier.

No one would ever know.

My family would never know. Conway would never know. I'd give her to Egor once he was finished with his business, and I could wipe my hands clean. My reputation would be intact.

But the guilt counteracted it. Back and forth, my conscience swayed.

We were talking about rape here.

I'd never been that kind of guy.

Did I want to start now?

Even if I didn't, I'd have to put her to use. If I didn't do something with her, she would find it suspicious that I bought her. She was smart, so she would push the envelope more and more. When she realized I wouldn't rape or kill her, she would understand what kind of power she had.

And then the chaos would erupt.

I could make her clean and cook, but I didn't need to pay fifty million for those services. Even if she wore lingerie at all times, I still didn't need to drop that kind of cash for that—and she would know it.

Fucking her seemed to be the only option.

But she would never want me. I would always have to use force.

Fuck.

I was sitting at my desk in my office when my phone started to ring.

Conway's name was on the screen.

My cousin was the last person I wanted to speak to right now after the stunt I'd just pulled. I'd dropped his name to get into the Underground, and I did something I promised I would never do.

What if he knew?

It was a bit ironic that he was calling me right now, especially in the morning. At this time of day, he was usually busy with Sapphire or working. I cleared my throat before I took the call. "What's up, Con?"

Silence. Heated silence.

That lack of response told me everything I needed to know.

Yep. He knew.

I didn't say anything else, knowing it would be stupid to say more than I should.

"I just had an interesting conversation." Anger spilled out over the phone, filling the air around me. It was hot and thick, humid like on a summer day.

"I hope you weren't talking to yourself."

"Carter," he hissed.

Bad time to make a joke.

"You went to the Underground and bought some woman—using my name?" The ferocity erupted over the line. "One of the Skull Kings called to check up on me because I've never sent someone in my place. Asked if I'd gotten the girl yet."

Maybe I should have given him a heads-up. "Look, I didn't know they were going to call you—"

"You don't know anything about the Underground. You don't know anything about the process. How stupid are you? You really thought you could pull this off without telling me? Do you have any idea how psycho the Skull Kings are?"

"To the best of my knowledge, they've never called you before."

"Because I've never sent you in my place, dumbass."

"And what did you say?"

He sighed into the phone. "I went with it. If I let them believe I was out of the loop, they would have killed you."

"Were you convincing?"

"Damn convincing, asshole. Now what the hell is going on, Carter? We promised we were out of the game. What could have possibly brought you back into it?"

"I didn't think I'd ever get back into it either. It was a one-time thing."

"And why was it a one-time thing?" He practically growled into the phone like a bear about to rip my face off. "What was so damn important that you would drag us back into this? I've got a wife now. And not just a wife—a pregnant wife. I can't risk her safety or the safety of my kid."

"I never wanted to drag you into it. I thought it would be simple—in and out."

"Asshole, it's never that simple. If you wanted this done right, you should have brought me into it."

"You would have said no."

"Damn right. And we wouldn't be in this mess because of my wisdom."

"Mess?" I asked. "What mess? They called and asked a few questions, and that was it. You're being paranoid."

"Am I?" he countered. "Because they've never called and asked questions before."

"That was because I've never gone in your place. Now that it's cleared up, we're good to go." The damage was done, and there was nothing we could do about it now anyway. "This is the last time, I swear."

He calmed down slightly, but his anger still

simmered. "What was so enticing that you couldn't say no?"

The only thing I cared about. "Cash."

"How much?"

"One-fifty."

Conway was silent, clearly surprised.

"I'll split it with you since you covered for me."

"Carter, I don't care about the money. I care about my family now. I want nothing to do with this anymore. Call me boring, but I want the quiet life that my father has always talked about. I want to wash my hands clean and start over."

"You're getting your wish. I only agreed because of the cash, but I won't agree again."

"You better not. And who offered you that kind of fortune?"

"Some Russian." I didn't want to tell Conway the specifics so he wouldn't worry. "Asked me to get his sister out. I said no at first, but he kept offering more and more money. When he hit one-fifty, I couldn't say no."

"One-fifty is a lot of money, but it's still not worth it. I want your promise that this is the last time."

"You've got my word, Con."

"And you can't give this woman back right away.

Skull Kings are paying attention. If they spot her some-where, we're done for."

"The Russian guy asked me to hold on to her for a month anyway. He's out of the country on business or something."

"Perfect. Keep her in the house."

Easier said than done. "She's a bit of a handful…"

"Why?" he countered. "Tell her she'll be rescued soon. Chill out and watch TV or something."

"Yeah…" I didn't tell him that Egor told me not to tell her he was coming for her. I knew I was in the middle of something I never should have gotten mixed up in. She definitely wasn't his sister, and whatever claim he had over her was sinister. I was curious to know what their real relationship was, but if I asked, I could get my hands even dirtier. It was best to be quiet, finish the job, and then forget about it. "Anyway, what are you and the wife doing?"

"No, we aren't gonna have a casual conversation like you didn't just cross me, Carter. I'm still pissed at you." Click. He hung up.

I set the phone on my desk and sighed, knowing I'd deserved that. Now that I had the woman in my house, understood that I was the middleman in a tense rela-tionship, I wished I could go back and deny Egor's offer. But something told me there would have been worse ramifications if I didn't cooperate.

Maybe doing what he asked was the best way to keep me and the rest of my family safe.

This woman was in a bad situation, but there was nothing anyone could do about it—especially me. I wouldn't bother asking her about her story. I wouldn't bother getting to know her at all. I would stay as distant from her as possible to make sure I never sympathized with her.

They say you should never get attached to the farm animals before they're slaughtered.

I'd follow that advice now.

FIFTEEN

Bones

———————

I walked into the bar, took a quick scan around, and found Max standing at the bar with a glass of scotch. One elbow rested on the counter, and his eyes were focused on a brunette on the opposite side of the room. With chiseled arms, battle scars, and an intense expression in his eyes, he was the kind of bad boy women were told to steer clear of.

But he was nothing compared to me.

It was my first night out in months, and the second I stood inside that room, I felt several women look my way. I was in a black t-shirt and jeans, the material hugging the rigid muscles of my body. All I'd been doing for the past few months was lifting weights and working, so my muscles bulged to their maximum capacity.

I made my way to the bar where Max was standing and took the spot beside him.

He tore his gaze away from the woman he was eyeing to look at me. His intense expression vanished when he saw me, his eyebrows rising up his forehead. His head cocked to the side slightly. "What are you doing here?"

"You invited me." I waved down the bartender, a pretty blonde, and got my usual.

"Yeah, but I didn't think you would come. You never come."

"Well, I did tonight." I clinked my glass against his and took a drink, letting the booze burn all the way down into my gut. Alcohol was an essential part of my life, and I would never take a hiatus from it again. But I would also never get that drunk again either.

Max's surprise faded away, and a boyish look of joy came over his face. "Finally, my boy is back." He clinked his glass against mine. "Damn, I missed you."

I chuckled and patted him on the back. "I missed you too."

"It's been a long three months," he said. "I wasn't sure if you would ever get over it."

I would never be over Vanessa completely, not when I loved her so deeply. But I'd finally come to accept that the relationship was really over and I

needed to move on with my life. She had moved on—
and now it was my turn.

"What brought you around?" he asked, taking a
drink from his glass.

"Acceptance. Closure."

His eyebrow arched with suspicion. "You didn't
drive out there, did you?"

I didn't answer by taking a drink.

"You drove all the way out there?" he asked incredulously. "What happened? Did you sleep with her or
something?"

No, I didn't even get out of my car. "I parked
outside her gallery and saw her inside."

"Oh no…"

"Relax. I saw her inside with some guy she was
seeing. They probably had dinner, and then they were
looking at her paintings together, holding hands. They
clearly have a relationship…not some fling."

Max's facial expression fell instantly, the sad horror
on his face. "Shit…are you alright?"

"Yeah." I looked into my glass, remembering the
searing pain inside my chest. "I was upset for a bit, but
then I realized I had no reason to be. We broke up for a
reason. She shouldn't be alone forever."

Max looked at me like he wasn't buying it.

"It gave me closure."

"Wow…who knew going out there would actually be a good idea."

"If she'd been alone in that gallery, I'm not sure what would have happened. Maybe I would have gotten out of the car. Maybe I wouldn't have. I don't know. Seeing her with someone else was probably the best thing that could have happened. It made me drive away. It made me come out to the bar with you. Something good came out of it."

He nodded in agreement. "True. I'm happy for you."

Happy wasn't the right word. I would never be as happy as I was when I was with her. Even when her family was insulting me every day, calling me trash, going home to her was the greatest part of my day. She was the only woman I would ever love. All the other women in my life would just be entertainment. "Yeah."

He drank from his glass then returned it to the counter. He looked at the booze, the dark liquid that made rational men turn into assholes. He sucked in his cheeks like he was soaking up every drop of scotch. He turned back to me again then patted his hand on the counter. "I wasn't going to tell you this because it's a conflict of interest, but since you're feeling better, I guess there's no harm."

The short spurt of peacefulness I'd felt was ruined

by what he said. My eyes darted to his face as my body tensed for whatever news he was about to share. "What?"

"I just got an offer for a hit. But I passed on it because it would be too weird."

Blood pounded in my temple just the way a migraine did. It thudded hard and deep, cracking my skull. My hand was on the cool glass, but now my fingertips didn't feel the cold sensation. All the chatter around me died away as my fear suffused the area around us. I was terrified of what he would say even though I had no idea what he would reveal. "Max, spit it out. Who's the target?"

He rubbed the back of his neck before he answered. "Conway Barsetti."

My blood turned ice-cold.

Fuck.

Now my heart pounded harder. My fear gripped both of my lungs so I couldn't breathe. I couldn't even think straight. All I thought about was Vanessa's heart-break as she attended her brother's funeral. I thought of the depression that would hit both of her parents, which would then destroy her. Her life would never be the same.

"I passed because I knew you wouldn't want any one of us to take the job."

"And you didn't think you should tell me this information anyway?" I slammed my drink onto the counter, making the glass shatter.

Max didn't flinch. "She's not part of your life anymore, Bones. It's none of your concern what happens to her or her family. She's got a new man now."

"None of my concern?" He was right, she wasn't my responsibility anymore. Her family had treated me like trash and took away the light of my life. They'd never treated me with respect or gave me a real chance. I should want them all to suffer. I should want them to lose someone they cared about, the way I lost someone I cared about. But none of those considerations entered my brain because they seemed irrelevant. All I thought about was Vanessa, the woman I loved. If I let this happen, she would never get over it. "It is my fucking concern. When did this happen? Who made the order?"

"I didn't get a lot of information. But it seems like the Skull Kings are behind it. Conway crossed them somehow, but they don't want to get their hands dirty because of his public image—which is why they called us."

"Jesus fucking Christ. When is this happening?"

"I'm not sure, but they offered a ton of cash, so I know someone will pick it up."

This was a damn nightmare. "Get that information. Now."

"What?" he asked incredulously. "What the hell are you going to do?"

"Make sure Conway doesn't get hit. Obviously."

"You can't be serious." Now he slammed his glass on the table. "After everything those stuck-up assholes did to you?"

"Irrelevant."

"Irrelevant? They treated you like scum."

"Because I am scum." I'd come to accept who I really was. I'd come to embrace it. "When it came down to it, Vanessa chose her family over me. That's because she can live without me, not without them. So if something happens to Conway or his wife, she'll never be the same. She'll know a new kind of heartbreak that she'll never recover from. I have to do something, Max. Now, get me that information. Not tomorrow or in an hour." I pointed my finger in his face. "You make those fucking calls right now."

MAX WAS SITTING on the couch in the living room with his laptop open. I was gathering all of my gear, my guns, ammo, bulletproof vest, everything I had. I had no idea who I was up against, and I had to be prepared.

Max hung up his call.

"What did you find out?" I barked.

"You aren't going to like it."

"Spit it out." I was ready to snap my rifle in half because I was so impatient.

"Conway has some appearance tonight in Milan. When he leaves, they're going to hit him then."

I glanced at the time on my watch. It was seven in the evening. That left only a few hours at most. "His wife?"

"She's at their house in Verona. But they're going to get her too. Take them both out."

"Fuck." I dragged my hand down my face, furious this was happening. "She's pregnant."

"I think that's the point."

I slammed my hand through the coffee table, smashing it and making a hole right through the wood.

Max didn't react. "You need to calm down."

"I won't fucking calm down." I was always calm on every mission. Nothing affected me because I was focused on my task. But this made the emotions inside me run haywire. This was personal now.

I pulled out my phone and called the man I thought I would never speak to again. A part of me hated him, hated him for the way he'd thrown me out like trash. But another part of me respected him, respected him for raising such a magnificent and strong daughter. I loved her so damn much, so I could never hate her father completely.

He picked up instantly, his guard sky-high. "What did I tell you?" He threatened me with just his tone of voice, reminding me what he would do to me if he ever saw me again. He'd pointed a gun right between my eyes and said he would kill me if I ever showed my face again. That was more than enough reason for me to let his son die. But my hatred for this man wasn't as strong as my love for his daughter.

"The Skull Kings have put a hit on Conway. I just found out thirty minutes ago. They're hitting Conway tonight at the banquet he's attending. They're also hitting Sapphire at their home in Verona. Their objective is to torture and kill them both."

Crow reacted far more calmly than I did when I first heard the news. Perhaps he was a seasoned veteran, someone who had the skill to remain logical when he should be emotional. "How do you know this?"

"We don't have time for this shit, alright? Everything I've said is factual. We have very little time here. You need to get Sapphire out and save Conway at the same time. Don't waste any more time talking to me."

Crow didn't question me, knowing he wouldn't call my bluff, not when his son's life was on the line. "The rest of my family. What about them?"

"No hits on any of them. They only want Conway and his wife." Vanessa was safe, the most important person on the list. If there were any chance she wasn't, I'd leave Conway to his fate and save her instead.

He hung up without saying anything else.

Not even thank you.

I shoved the phone into my pocket. I was tempted to call Vanessa, but there wasn't time for that. After not speaking to her for so long, the conversation wouldn't be simple and short. She was in no danger, so there was no point in telling her anything. "Call the guys. They'll get Sapphire out of there. You and I will take care of Conway."

Max gave me the most dumbfounded expression I'd ever seen. "You can't be serious. You expect us to risk our lives for those assholes? After what they did to you?" He rose to his feet. "After we've had to see you mope around for the last three months and almost die in a car accident?"

"I'm not doing it for them. I'm doing it for her."

"Whatever," he snapped. "Her life isn't on the line, so I couldn't care less."

"Max." If I had to do this alone, I would. But my chances of success were much greater with my crew. "They're all five hours away. They probably have men around here, and they can probably get here in a chopper, but still. They need me."

"Did they ask for your help?"

"No. But that doesn't matter."

"I think it does."

"Max, together or apart, Vanessa is my second." When it came to our partners, it was a mutual understanding that they were the priority of us all. If Cynthia's mother were kidnapped, we'd all be involved. "She's still my second. She'll always be my second."

Max's nostrils flared in annoyance, but he finally dropped the argument.

"I've gotta do this, Max. I know Vanessa…if she loses her brother, she'll never get over it."

"I don't see how that's your problem, man. She turned her back on you."

But she didn't want to. I remembered the last day we were together, the way she was broken like shattered glass. I'd never seen her lose her strength like that, seen her sob like that. Losing me was the hardest thing she'd ever had to do. I knew she still loved me, even if she was with someone else. I knew she would never love him the way she loved me. "Even if she did, I would never turn my back on her."

Max sighed, his eyes dropping their hostility. He moved his hands to his hips, staring at me with indecision in his eyes. He considered the task before him through several heartbeats.

"I need an answer, Max. I have to get going."

He dropped his hands and picked up the bulletproof vest from the table. He started to strap it on. "I'm in. But not for them—for you."

Also by Penelope Sky

The story continues in…

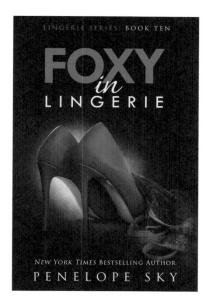

Order Now

Made in the USA
Thornton, CO
08/16/24 10:49:00

17150376-f3c8-46c7-858a-d61fdc2f5ab1R01